STAR WARS

THE RISE OF SKYWALKER

by Michael Kogge

Screenplay by Chris Terrio & J.J. Abrams

Story by Derek Connolly & Colin Trevorrow
and Chris Terrio & J.J. Abrams

DISNEY

LUCASFILM
PRESS

Los Angeles • New York

Printed in the United States of America

First Edition, April 2020
1 3 5 7 9 10 8 6 4 2
FAC-029261-20073

Library of Congress Control Number on file
ISBN 978-1-368-05426-3

Visit the official *Star Wars* website at: www.starwars.com.

SUSTAINABLE
FORESTRY
INITIATIVE

Certified Sourcing

www.sfiprogram.org
SFI-01054
The SFI label applies to the text stock

The dead speak! The galaxy has heard a mysterious broadcast, a threat of REVENGE in the sinister voice of the late EMPEROR PALPATINE.

GENERAL LEIA ORGANA dispatches secret agents to gather intelligence, while REY, the last hope of the Jedi, trains for battle against the diabolical FIRST ORDER.

Meanwhile, Supreme Leader KYLO REN rages in search of the phantom Emperor, determined to destroy any threat to his power....

PROLOGUE

ONCE THERE WAS a woman who was born to lead. Orphaned as a child, she was adopted by royalty and became a princess of a peaceful planet. She began a life of public service as an outspoken Imperial senator, later becoming a commander in the Rebel Alliance, a politician in the New Republic, and then the head of the Resistance in the fight against the First Order. When she was a young rebel, she discovered the dark truth about her heritage. Her name was Leia, and by birth she was a Skywalker. But she never took that name for her own. In the galaxy she was always known as an Organa.

Once there was an old man who wanted never to die. He came from the nobility of an affluent world and was elected to lead the Old Republic through its gravest crisis, as its chancellor. His name was Palpatine, and he was often described as a thin, kindly gentleman who harbored no ambition other than to bring stability to a war-torn galaxy. But another ambition he did have, one so cunning and sinister that few realized it until after he had turned the Republic into an Empire and declared himself Emperor. By this title alone he became known, as his own name slipped into the recesses of the past, along with knowledge of the Republic's most stalwart guardians, the Jedi Knights, whose extermination he engineered. With no one to oppose him, he held the entire galaxy under his command. Only mortality stood in the way of eternal rule, though even that might be overcome if he discovered the ancient secrets. It was at the height of his power, when all seemed secure, that the unforeseen happened. His own apprentice turned against him, throwing him to his death and thereby helping topple his Empire.

Once there was a boy who was born with an extraordinary gift. He could hear things, see things, and do things others could not. His mother shared a similar gift, as did his uncle, but not his father. What was special about the boy's gift was that he heard voices from time to time. The voices told him secret things and warned him when he was in danger. He did as the voices instructed and told no one else about them, not his parents or his uncle, who trained him to join a new order of Jedi Knights. As the boy grew older, the voices faded from his dreams until he forgot about them altogether. But their influence remained. He eventually spurned his uncle's teachings and used his gift not for good but for evil. His parents had named him Ben, but the name he took for himself was Kylo Ren.

Once there was a girl who had many dreams. One of them was to become a pilot and see the stars. In preparation, she practiced endlessly on flight simulators and built her own speeders from scavenged parts. She also dreamed of the past. She read, watched, and listened to everything she could about the Jedi of old, who had mythic powers that defied belief. But as much as she imagined herself flying starships and learned stories of mystical warriors from mysterious worlds, she could not explore the universe beyond the desert planet where she'd been orphaned. She had to wait until her parents returned. Her name was Rey, born of a family she did not know.

One day events beyond her control forced the girl to leave her desert home. She copiloted a famous starship under its celebrated captain, who told her that the Jedi and their powers were more than a myth. She also discovered that she had the gift to become one of their number if she received the proper training. When the last of the Jedi failed to teach her what she needed, she turned to another, a woman who had received the training but followed a different vocation.

So under Leia Organa's tutelage, Rey learned the ways of the Jedi.

CHAPTER 1

THE JUNGLE WAS ALIVE, and Rey was alive with it.

She darted through the dense brush, never stopping, never slowing. She dipped under half-hidden branches and hopped over exposed roots. She brushed a webweaver off her shoulder and dodged the flick of a zymond's poisonous tongue. When she came upon swampy ground, she grabbed a creeper vine and swung over it. Her breathing remained steady throughout and she didn't break a sweat, despite the humidity. Rey might have been a creature of the desert, accustomed to the sand and sun of Jakku, but on Ajan Kloss she moved through the jungle as if she'd lived there her whole life.

Such was the power of the Force. For those who opened themselves up to it, even the most foreign environments could become like home.

As fast as she ran, however, Rey could not shake off her pursuers. They whizzed through the air behind her, four combat remotes—one blue, one white, one green, and one red—targeting her with stingbeams. Though she couldn't sense the robotic devices the same way she could living organisms, she was able to track them by discerning how they interacted with their surroundings. The chrome of their surfaces made glittering reflections in rainwater puddles. The puff of their maneuvering jets quieted the noisy tree chirpers. And the beams of their lasers emitted the scorched scent of ozone. All these sights, sounds, and smells clued Rey into the remotes' locations so she could stay one step ahead of them and their precisely timed shots.

She had another pursuer, a friendly one, who whined while struggling to keep pace. Colored orange and white, with a domed head and a spherical body, the astromech droid BB-8 was designed for starship maintenance and hyperspace navigation, not high-speed chases through wild jungles. The uneven land and thick vegetation made travel challenging for a mechanical being that rolled rather than walked or flew. Still, using every gadget available to an astromech, BB-8 managed to stay within beeping distance.

Rey had told her little friend to stay back at the base, but of course, BB-8 had refused. The droid was, above all else, stubbornly loyal. But the remotes weren't going to quit because her unwanted helper lagged behind. They kept zapping at her while she kept running toward her goal, lightsaber hilt in hand. Their laser beams could inflict a nasty sting, as their name implied, but Rey wasn't worried so much about the pain as she was about slowing down. Every second was precious if she wanted to impress her teacher and achieve a personal best.

She snagged a branch that blocked her way, vaulted over it, and then snapped it back at the remotes. The branch smashed into the white remote and hurled it into the bushes. A beam from the blue remote singed the air over her as she ducked and instead struck its green counterpart, causing the electronic device to fizzle and die. She took care of the blue remote by blowing on a fanged flower that she dashed past. Alerted by her breath, its petal mouth did the rest, snatching the orb from the air.

When Rey came to the edge of a gorge, she didn't pause to get her bearings. Following her teacher's instructions, she picked up an old A-wing pilot's helmet from a tree stump and jammed it over her head. Rey pulled the helmet's blast shield over her eyes and then did something that made BB-8 shriek so loudly Rey heard it through the helmet's mufflers.

She ignited her lightsaber and stepped onto the tightrope bridge that spanned the gorge.

The red remote whistled after her. Blind as Rey might be with her eyes, she wasn't blind in the Force. Though she couldn't see the remote, she knew where it was in connection with everything else and could anticipate its next moves. When it fired at her from behind, she batted away its shots with her lightsaber blade. Coming to the end of the tightrope, she jumped onto firm ground and tossed off the helmet. She didn't bother to glance back at her pursuer but immediately went to work climbing a giant broadleaf tree.

From an upper branch fluttered a piece of red ribbon. It would be hers.

As she neared the ribbon, the red remote swooped toward the tree. Rey launched herself off the tree and sliced the ribbon with her saber as she fell. The red remote's beam missed her and shredded the end of the ribbon instead.

Her boots thudded on the ground but didn't stay there for long. She tucked the ribbon in her sash and ran across the tightrope, her capelet fanning out behind her. BB-8 met her on the other side of the gorge and sped after her, offering congratulatory beeps. She was going to pass this test in record time. The general would be proud.

Then Rey stopped, her heels kicking up dirt and leaves. Hovering before her was the red remote. Its maneuvering jets hissed at her. The blasted thing was tenacious, she had to give it that. But it was time to end this game.

The blue blade she held had once been wielded by Luke Skywalker and his father before him. It had been damaged on more than one occasion, most recently in Supreme Leader Snoke's throne room. The kyber crystal that powered the blade had shattered when she and Kylo Ren had fought for the weapon. But Rey had retrieved its pieces, and through a careful study of the texts she had taken from Ahch-To, she had mended the crystal and rebuilt the lightsaber.

Nonetheless, before she could bring the blade up in front of her, the remote hit her in the shoulder with a stingbeam. She winced, but the pain could have been worse. That beam was on a lower setting. The red remote was toying with her.

The next round of shots bounced off her blade and were sent back at the remote. In each case, the remote dodged the bolts, but while it was tracking the deflected beams, it couldn't track her.

Or so she thought.

As she tried to run past the remote, a tightly focused stingbeam struck her before she realized it had been fired. She shuddered, not so much from the pain but from frustration. There was no way—just *no way*—a training remote was going to get the better of her.

She lunged at it.

The remote evaded her attack, looping around her and unleashing more blasts. The majority of the shots she deflected, but a couple got through. Those stung—and the pain didn't fade away. The remote had increased the intensity of its beams.

Now she was angry.

Rey swung wildly at the remote. She'd broken a sweat. She was breathing hard. Her blue blade cut through tree after tree, toppling them without regard. The remote remained just out of reach, pelting her with lasers. Each new hit stung more than the last, yet the pain also energized her. She'd bring down the jungle on the mechanical pest if she had to.

The red remote soared up and around her. Venting her frustration, she hurled her lightsaber at it. Though her blade came close to striking its mark, the remote rotated its jets to thrust away from the saber's arc. The blade chopped through the treetops, carving a window to the sky.

Rey whirled, searching for the remote. It reeled and dove at her from behind. It was done toying with her—its high-pitched whine signified its next stingbeam would do more than sting. She'd be knocked to the ground, her muscles stunned. Her efforts to beat her previous best would have been for naught.

The remotes had all been programmed to analyze her combat moves and forecast her probable actions. Up to this point, the red remote had made an exceptional number of correct predictions. Yet for all its success, it lacked the capability to estimate one most crucial factor.

The Force.

As a consequence, the red remote never calculated that a falling branch would upend the laws of gravity and hurtle into Rey's hand. Wielding it as she would her staff, she whacked the remote backward into a tree. The red globe shattered on impact, leaving a dent in the trunk.

Rey let out a breath. She dropped the branch and caught her lightsaber hilt as it fell to the ground, its blade having switched off mid-arc.

She had broken her old record. Yet she felt no joy in her accomplishment. Around her, gigantic trees that had stood for centuries lay on the forest floor as fallen logs. The very life that had supported her in the Force had ended with her blade.

Her actions mortified her. It would have been better to lose the remote than do such grave harm to the jungle. She would return to her teacher not triumphant but ashamed.

Before she could take a step back toward the Resistance base, she froze, assaulted by a vision.

She glimpsed a young man meditating over a burnt black mask. He lifted his head as if noticing her. The young man was Kylo Ren, and the mask was that of his grandfather Darth Vader.

Rey's surroundings shifted to a large, dark chamber. Before her was a mound of spikes resembling an enormous Jakku sand urchin. A cloaked figure sat on a throne in the center of the spikes. She couldn't tell who it was. But there was a familiarity in it. Again, could it be . . .

Kylo Ren?

He had been there, was there, or would be there. She felt the echoes of his presence. His anger. His fury. His soul, forever at war. Somehow he was connected to all this.

Memories intruded. The first was one from her worst nightmare, of the time as a child when she had watched her parents' starship launch from the desert sands, forever abandoning her on Jakku. Yet she also remembered a moment she'd never remembered before and found herself locked in the warm embrace of a woman who could only be her mother. She would have stayed in that moment forever, but Kylo Ren interrupted it. He stood on the Mega-Destroyer, the body of Supreme Leader Snoke at his feet, and extended his hand to her.

Join me. . . .

The voice wasn't Ren's. It was deeper than his and rasped, as if whoever spoke struggled to breathe.

Master Luke came to her next, standing on the island cliff in his brown robes, as he had when she first found him.

After him there was Han Solo, her mentor for only a few days, but whose encouragement had led Rey to Leia and the Resistance. She saw Han touching his son's face, before that same son plunged a lightsaber blade into his chest. *You did it,* she heard Master Luke say. *You killed him.* And then she was thrown back into the dark chamber. Dim lighting gave definition to the hooded figure on the throne. It wasn't Kylo Ren.

The face she saw terrified her.

A beep, muted and muffled, rescued her from seeing more. She blinked and was in the jungle once again, standing among the fallen trees. Under one trunk squealed BB-8, his servomotors grinding in a futile attempt to escape. The poor thing. Her thoughtless rampage with the lightsaber had gotten him trapped beneath a tree and had popped loose a panel, exposing his internal circuitry.

She rushed over to him. "I'm so sorry." As she pulled him out, he didn't complain, only expressed worry about her. Was she okay? Had she had another vision?

"Yes, it happened to me again." She didn't want to go into details.

But BB-8 wasn't the kind of droid you could dismiss when it came to the safety of his friends. His beeps kept coming. What had she seen? Was the Force telling her something?

"No, I still don't know what the Force was trying to show me. But this time," she said, "this time was worse."

Growing up an orphan on Jakku, Rey had always had the most vivid dreams and nightmares, so vivid they felt real. But one nightmare in particular had recurred more than the others. It had haunted her not only in her sleep but when she was awake, and it had just haunted her in her latest vision. It was the cruelest moment of her childhood, when she had screamed in Unkar Plutt's grip while her parents left Jakku, never to return. Though the double thruster engines of their starship burned blue in her memory as if they had blazed only the day before, she couldn't remember the faces of her parents anymore. All she could remember was a voice.

Stay here. I'll come back for you, sweetheart. I promise.

She never could figure out whether the voice belonged to her mother or her father—or both. It didn't matter; all that mattered was the promise to come back for her. So for years she had heeded the voice's command, remaining on Jakku, scavenging scrap for food portions and marking each passing day on the wall of her Imperial walker home.

The voice was part of her past. When she had clashed with Kylo Ren on the Mega-Destroyer, he had told her that her parents were nothing but junk traders who sold her off for drinking money. Although she knew Ren was a master of lies—even lying to himself about his identity as Ben Solo—what he had said didn't feel like a lie. It felt like the truth.

The confrontation had made her acknowledge that the voice she had been hearing all those years was nothing more than a defense mechanism—a hope she had invented for herself so she would not give in to despair and could survive a difficult situation, which life on Jakku undoubtedly had been. While trying to hurt and confuse her, Ren had inadvertently forced her to reckon with her past. She needn't wait for her parents to show up when deep down she knew they never would. She had found a family of her own in the Resistance. Her friends, like Finn, General Organa, Chewbacca, and BB-8, cared about her, as she cared about them. And since her acceptance of her new life, the voice and that dream hadn't disturbed her again.

She still had other dreams, however, and these were more like waking nightmares. They showed her dark places she did not know, strange figures she did not recognize, and ominous events she did not understand. She tried to follow her teacher's advice and reach out through the Force to the Jedi who had come before her, for direction. "Let go of all thought. Let go of fear. Invite them to be with you, and you will hear them. They can give you guidance," Leia had said.

But as much as Rey tried to reach out, she hadn't heard a peep or felt a hint that Luke or any other Jedi were out there. There was nothing but silence. What Leia was asking her to do seemed impossible.

"Nothing's impossible," Leia had told her time and again.

If nothing was impossible, why couldn't Rey stop these visions from haunting her?

"Let's go back," Rey said. BB-8 didn't question her this time.

CHAPTER 2 \\\\\

MUSTAFAR WAS A WORLD of hot spots and groundquakes, volcanoes and fissures. A world with an unstable core that cracked continents and spewed fire through those cracks. A world where lava flowed in rivers and ash fell like rain. A world seemingly angry with itself.

It was a world where Kylo Ren should have felt at home.

Upon arrival, however, he felt nothing of the sort. This red-hot world, where Anakin Skywalker had died and Darth Vader had ruled, had begun to cool.

Where there should have been death, there was life. A thicket of irontrees had sprouted in the once-molten plains near his grandfather's castle. A band of rag-garbed, goggle-wearing colonists known as the Alazmec surrounded the thicket, defiantly raising crude weapons as if they were the trees' sacred protectors.

Ren and his squad of stormtroopers stood a few meters away from the defenders. "Bow to the Supreme Leader of the First Order, Kylo Ren," declared the stormtrooper captain, "or be destroyed."

The colonists' goggles flickered like a constellation of

stars. One among them screeched from under a burlap scarf. Ren picked up enough words to understand the meaning. *We bow only to one, the Dark Lord, the true father and ruler of the galaxy. Vader.*

These Alazmec were pilgrims, having ventured to Mustafar to honor Darth Vader. Though the Dark Lord had perished a generation before, the fear he had inspired proved so deep-rooted that cults had sprung up worshiping him, just as they had for the Jedi and their twisted view of the Force.

"If you bow to Vader," Ren told them, "you bow to me."

His black cloak billowed behind him. His hair, stringy and dark, caught ashes in the wind. His eyes, taking in all his opponents, did not blink. Most recognized Kylo Ren by his mask, but he glared at the Alazmec with his human face. It was scarred and cruel and perhaps more frightening than anything he could wear, because it showed he was real and his power was real.

A few of the Alazmec wavered, but none bowed. If they would not recognize his power, he would have to teach them. Ren marched toward them and ignited his lightsaber.

Scarlet plasma burst from the hilt, one long beam for the blade, two smaller beams for the crossguard. All crackled like trapped flames, barely contained. He had built the saber himself, using a fractured kyber crystal to energize the beams. Its instability made wielding the weapon like playing with fire. Ren had designed it that way. He'd been playing with fire most of his life. He was the fire.

The Alazmec outnumbered him many times over, but that only gave him more lives to end. Their scatter blasters, clubs, axes, and metal swords were no match for his blade. Those who tried to run from him didn't get far. His stormtroopers took care of them with their rifles.

The fight was over all too soon. He whirled but found no more Alazmec to kill. Their bodies lay scattered in the dirt around the trees. Not a single one of them survived.

The stormtroopers lowered their blasters. Ren did not retract his blade. He still felt the stain of life—not the dull mindlessness of the irontrees but a being that was strong, intelligent, cunning. It called to him, a low rumble coming from a dense grove of trees.

Ren strode toward the sound, lightsaber in hand. Whatever it was might be able to tell the truth about the recent transmission that had shaken the galaxy.

At last, the work of generations is complete. The great error is corrected. The day of victory is at hand. The day of revenge. The day of the Sith.

The transmission was short, sent from an old Imperial communications hub across the galaxy, from the Core to the Outer Rim. There was much deliberation about what it meant and its age. Most assumed it was a remnant of the Imperial days and was resurfacing as a trick. But the voice in the message was undeniable. Analysts confirmed that the one who had spoken those words was none other than Emperor Palpatine, believed dead for three decades.

The broadcast bolstered the rumors that he still lived

but was in hiding, waiting to return. And if the Emperor was indeed alive, many in the First Order thought he should be the one in control, not Kylo Ren.

Ren would not let that happen. He would root out this Emperor and kill him, just as he had killed his former master, Supreme Leader Snoke. Then there would be no debate about who commanded the First Order.

Mustafar had seemed a plausible location to look for answers. The dark side was strong on this world—so strong that Ren's grandfather had built his castle there.

Ren walked into the center of a grove where mists circled a peaty bog. Marshland shouldn't exist on a volcanic world, yet there it was, reeking of the dark side. Partially submerged in the muck was a massive humanoid head, completely hairless with pointed ears, closed eyes, and a piglike nose. A spidery creature of many eyes and many limbs crowned the head. With long legs gripping the sides, the creature had partially inserted itself into the skull, and its abdomen throbbed as it fed on its host's brain.

Ren kept his saber lit. Mustafarian myths told of an oracle who dwelled in a hidden swamp and possessed the ability to tell the future. Could this be it, the fabled Eye of Webbish Bog?

"Ssseed of Ssskywalker," it hissed. Ren nearly buried his blade in the creature right then. He would never answer to that name. But he maintained control and let the oracle continue. "You have defeated my protectors, and so you have earned my wisdom." The oracle moved one of its legs, and as if pulled by a puppet string, the host's gigantic five-fingered hand emerged from the mud. One rubbery finger pointed beyond the bog. The mists parted, and through a gap in the irontrees, Ren saw the ruins of Lord Vader's fortress.

"In the castle of your kin there is a domain of darkness. There you will find an ancient wayfinder," the oracle said as Ren stared at the ruins. "That wayfinder will reveal a path to one you seek. Be warned—secrets weary of their tyranny."

When Ren looked back, the Eye of Webbish Bog and the immense head it sat on had sunk into the mud. A belch of surface bubbles was the only proof Ren had not imagined it.

Ren tread carefully around the bog and walked out of the irontree grove. He crossed the plains that smoked from cooling magma and approached the castle. Once it had stood tall and straight, a central obsidian tower flanked by two angled spires. Now the castle lay in shambles, blasted apart. And the dark side drifted around it like phantom wisps.

Like a hunter on a trail, Ren followed the wisps through the ruins, guided only by his instincts. He pictured himself in his grandfather's boots, red saber in hand, unafraid of anyone or anything, the galaxy in his grasp. Ren would have given anything to meet the great man, just once. But not as Anakin, as Luke Skywalker had called him. Anakin Skywalker was a coward and a traitor. Darth Vader was Ren's true grandfather.

Ren reached out with the Force on the chance that, as the pilgrims claimed, Vader's ghost haunted the ruins.

No one answered his call.

The wisps led Ren to an area where irontrees had sprouted. Most of the rubble had been cleared away except for a cracked column atop which rested a stone ark. Ren sensed immediately he was on hallowed ground. Vader had spent many hours in meditation there, pondering the future and plotting revenge against his enemies.

Perhaps he had foreseen his grandson finding the ark one day. Perhaps he had even left a message.

The ark bore no handles or knobs, for the key to opening it was nothing physical. Ren put his hands on the lid and gave it a hard shove with the Force. The lid fell to smash onto the ground.

Ren reached inside the ark and pulled out a small object shaped like a pyramid. Navigational symbols had been etched on each of its glassy sides. A sickly green glow emanated from its center.

From his studies under Snoke, Ren had learned that the ancient Sith and Jedi had used triangular devices called wayfinders to chart courses to worlds unreachable by normal means. They had done this by imparting each wayfinder with a touch of the Force. The one he held must have been his grandfather's wayfinder, for Vader's anger pulsed in the dark side like a raw nerve.

Exegol.

Kylo Ren knew where he had to go.

CHAPTER 3

KYLO REN STEERED his TIE whisper through the churning red gases of an exploded star. The slant-winged interceptor was superfast and state-of-the-art, one of a few designed by First Order engineers personally for him. But what mattered most on this journey was his grandfather's wayfinder. Without the coordinates it fed to his navicomputer, no measure of speed, skill, or even the Force would have allowed Ren to survive the treacherous path into the Unknown Regions.

He emerged in the lonely Exegol system. A murky blue haze shrouded the moonless planet. Ren followed the wayfinder's coordinates and landed the fighter on the barren surface. As he climbed out of the TIE, crackling lightning revealed a fortress of black stone floating before him.

Ren walked toward it, igniting his lightsaber. When he went under the citadel, the ground beneath him moved, and he descended on a stone disk into an abyss.

Statues had been chiseled into the rock walls around him. He recognized some of them from his studies. Locphet,

Mindran, Sissiri, Felkor, Sadow. All lords of the dark side. All Sith. Their mouths did not move, but he heard their unintelligible whispers.

He also heard a voice familiar to him since childhood. Throaty like a wet cough, it used to terrify him. "At last," the voice said, sounding both close and far away. "Snoke trained you well."

The lift came to a rest. Ren stepped off and looked for the speaker. "I killed Snoke," he said. "I'll kill you."

Seeing no one, he walked down a passage. Fluorescent light flickered from faulty panels. Fissures in the floor crackled with electricity from an energy storm that roiled far below.

"My boy, I made Snoke," the voice continued. "I have been every voice"—its tone shifted to inflect the snarl of the dead Supreme Leader and then the deep bass of Ren's grandfather—"you have ever heard inside your head."

The revelation confirmed Ren's suspicion that the voices in his head had originated from a single source. Just as he had tormented Darth Vader, the Emperor had tormented Ren.

That torment would end today. Ren would finish what his grandfather had started and kill the wretch once and for all.

Ren went forward, saber raised, into a laboratory. Hooded beings operated strange equipment, ignoring him. Beakers and pipettes lay on stained workbenches. Jars on shelves preserved what looked like human brains. A giant tank contained naked creatures with pinched eyes and shriveled flesh. As Ren passed the tank, he glimpsed a face.

It was the face of Snoke.

The Snoke Ren had killed hadn't been much of a supreme leader at all. Only an organism grown in a vat that could have been replaced. Ren had been right to seize control of the First Order from him.

"The First Order was just the beginning," the voice said, as if reading Ren's thoughts. "I will give you so much more."

Ren turned, looking for the speaker. "You'll die first."

"I have died before." One of the machines rotated toward him. Lightning flashed to divulge a decrepit old man in the grip of a clawlike harness. Glimpsed under a shadowy hood, his face had the pallor of a corpse. His eyes were clouded, and many of his teeth had rotted. He wore the same simple black robes he had once worn during his rare public outings, yet it wasn't his appearance that convinced Ren he was not an imposter. It was the evil he emanated, an evil so cold and lonely that it could only have come from the one who had controlled his grandfather.

The transmission had been authentic. Emperor Palpatine had subverted death and returned. But how?

The old man answered Ren's unspoken question. "The dark side of the Force is a pathway to many abilities some consider to be . . . unnatural."

Ren swung his saber toward the old man's wrinkled face. "What could you give me?"

Palpatine did not flinch from Ren's blade. "Everything." He lifted his crippled hands toward Ren, his flesh pocked by decay. "A new Empire."

The equipment in the laboratory began to rattle from a distant rumbling. Palpatine grinned at Ren. "The might of the Final Order will soon be ready."

Monitors in the laboratory switched from experimental readouts to show images of weapon-laden, gray-hulled Star Destroyers rising through the cracked surface. Ren was startled. Did the Emperor have his own war fleet on Exegol? Was this where all the remaining Imperial ships had fled after the Battle of Jakku? If Ren added this fleet to his own, no one would dare rebel against his authority as Supreme Leader of the First Order.

"It will be yours if you do what I ask," the old man said.

Ren kept his lightsaber pointed at Palpatine. But he did not strike him down. Not yet. Ren wanted whatever secrets this old man knew. He wanted control of the fleet.

Palpatine's smile broadened. "Kill the girl. End the Jedi. And become what your grandfather Vader could not," he said, exhaling an icy breath. "You will rule all the galaxy as the new emperor. But beware. She is not who you think she is."

Ren's hold on his lightsaber quivered. Snoke had told him much about the scavenger named Rey—and Ren had learned more himself when he had ripped memories from her mind. But was there something else about her? Something he had missed? Something she had hidden?

"Who is she?" he asked.

Palpatine chuckled and told Ren a secret he would have never guessed.

In the cave that housed the Resistance base, Rey had partitioned out a workshop where she could study, meditate, and tinker. She stayed there after her failure in the jungle, looking through the Jedi texts she had taken from Ahch-To. *Death is not a final departure,* one unnamed author had written, *for those whom you revere can return to you, at the time of your greatest need.*

Rey calmed herself and stretched out with her feelings. She knew Master Luke could help her understand her visions, if she could reach him. So she imagined him as she had last seen him, standing in the rain on that windswept island, watching her board the *Falcon* to leave Ahch-To.

But like the many times she had tried before, she felt and heard nothing.

Her attempts to contact him ended when she was called to see the general. BB-8 led the way to the base's command center, where her teacher waited.

"Beebee-Ate says you had a vision during your training exercise. What did you see?" Leia asked.

"I wish I knew. It . . ." Rey hesitated, not wanting to recall her vision. None of it made any sense, and it might needlessly worry her teacher.

A small woman who cast a large shadow, General Leia

Organa maintained dress and decorum even in dank places like this jungle cave. She kept her graying hair in a classic Alderaanian style and wore a stiff-collared sea-blue coat over royal purple robes. She didn't appear bothered by the stuffy, sticky air that made Rey itch. And she was endowed with an intensity unlike anyone Rey had ever met. If Leia asked a question, she expected an answer.

"I'm listening," she said.

Lacking an explanation, Rey looked around the cave. Life flourished in a variety of forms. Roots drooped from the ceiling. Fungi grew on the walls. Worms crawled in the dirt where lizards scurried. And nothing was out of reach of the creeper vines. They had snaked themselves around the holo-consoles, the crates that doubled as tables and chairs, and the hull of the *Tantive IV*, a CR90 blockade runner that was parked inside the cave and provided a power source for the command center.

Rey saw no easy way out of the conversation. She couldn't ignore the woman who had done so much for her, spending her precious time teaching Rey what she knew of the Force and the Jedi. Many of Leia's lessons came from her twin brother, Master Luke Skywalker himself, who had tutored his sister decades before. Though Leia's life had diverged from becoming a Jedi, she had never closed herself off to the Force as her brother had. She allowed the Force to be a guiding hand in her decisions, she had told Rey, even though she seldom spoke to others about her gift.

Her latest decision seemed to have taken Rey's education

into account. Out of all the planets in the galaxy, the general had relocated the remaining members of the Resistance to an old Rebel Alliance outpost on Ajan Kloss, where Luke had trained her years earlier. Rey didn't want Leia to regret the decision because of any dark visions Rey was having. She might stop teaching Rey out of fear, as Luke had done on Ahch-To.

"It was nothing," Rey said. "Nothing I could make out. It looked like a blur, like flashes of light—"

"I don't want to know what things look like," Leia interrupted. "I want to know what they *are*."

"I know. I think . . ." Rey searched for the right words to end this. "I'm just tired, that's all."

It was a poor excuse and Rey knew it. Yet before Leia could press her further, Lieutenant Connix strode over to them. "General?"

Unlike Leia, Connix's outfit was more suited for the jungle. She wore a light jacket over beige drabs, as did many of her peers. She had her hair tied in a braid around her head, matching the holos Rey had seen of young Princess Leia during the Battle of Endor. The lieutenant likely had chosen this style not only because it was practical but out of admiration for the general she adored. Rey knew Leia felt the same for Connix.

"We're getting reports of First Order activity around Sinta. We don't have confirmation yet since the *Falcon* is still in transit to the mining colony," Connix said. "The commander's asking for guidance."

Chewbacca, Poe Dameron, and Finn had taken the *Millennium Falcon* on a secret mission to Sinta Glacier Colony after the Resistance had received an urgent request from one of its top informants, a mining supervisor named Boolio. Rey hadn't been keen on the idea of Poe flying the freighter, despite having bonded with him on their journey to Minfar. Poe might be the best pilot in the Resistance, but with Han Solo gone, the *Falcon* had come under her and Chewbacca's care. She didn't want Poe wrecking the ship while trying one of the daredevil stunts he had a reputation for pulling.

At least Chewie was with them as copilot. He'd look out for the *Falcon*. And Rey knew she shouldn't be concerned about Poe when she had failed her own test in the jungle. Before she could criticize others, she needed to rectify her mistakes.

Rey handed Leia her lightsaber. "I will earn your brother's saber," she said, "one day." She felt she didn't deserve to carry the weapon of a Jedi after she had allowed her impatience to influence her actions.

Taking the saber, Leia showed neither surprise nor disappointment. Rey assumed BB-8 had told Leia about what had happened in the jungle, though whatever Leia thought about it she kept to herself. Leia rarely commented on Rey's performance. She preferred to let Rey make her own judgments, which was a frustrating way to learn. It made it difficult to distinguish between what was right and what was wrong.

Rotating around Rey, BB-8 made his opinion known with a beep. "No," Rey said. "You can't do it for me."

About to leave with Connix, Leia turned to Rey. "Never underestimate a droid."

"Yes, Master," Rey said, and watched Leia walk away.

BB-8 tooted a question. Rey crouched down to his level. "I couldn't tell her the truth," she whispered. "Who knows what she'd think if I did."

The droid grumbled and crooked his dome at her, as if suspicious.

"No, I tell you everything." She stood and gestured for him to follow. "Let's get you fixed."

That seemed to satisfy BB-8, at least for the moment. He rolled alongside her, babbling in binary, voicing a new concern about Finn and the others.

"Oh, don't worry about them. I'm sure our friends are fine."

As for herself, however, Rey had doubts.

CHAPTER 4

FINN WATCHED CHEWBACCA, looking for any telltale sign of his next move. As a species, Wookiees were quite demonstrative with their emotions. But when it came to playing holochess, Chewbacca seemed unreadable.

The three-dimensional creatures flickered on the *Millennium Falcon*'s game board. Several minutes had passed since Finn and Poe made their move, and Poe shifted in the wraparound lounge seats, leaning toward Chewbacca. "Are you ever going to go?"

Chewbacca glanced at Poe, then returned to examining the board, refusing to be rushed.

"He can't beat us every time," Finn said to Poe, in a conspiratorial whisper meant for Chewbacca to hear. But it didn't distract the Wookiee. It confounded Finn that Chewie could focus so intensely on the pieces yet abandon all self-control when he lost his temper. "How does he do it?"

"It's because he cheats," Poe said.

This provoked a defensive roar that made Poe crack a smile. "I'm kidding! You're two hundred and fifty years old. Of course you're better than us!"

Finn spoke over his friend. "Come on, take your turn. You're taking forever—that's why we think you're cheating!"

The autopilot chimed that they were nearing the Sinta Glacier Colony. Chewbacca rose from the board, growling at the two of them.

"Don't worry," Finn said, waving his hands as if to calm the Wookiee down.

"We're not going to turn it off," Poe added.

After the Wookiee thumped out of the lounge, Finn glanced at Poe. "He's cheating."

"Definitely." Poe touched a button on the holochess table and the pieces disappeared.

The two went out into the main corridor, where an armless Trodatome named Klaud was bending his tubular body toward a sparking panel. General Organa had denied Poe's request to have Rey join them on the mission and assigned them Klaud instead. No one understood a word Klaud said, but he seemed mechanically minded, so Poe put him to work making repairs around the ship.

"Klaud, I hope you fixed that surge." Poe gave him a hearty slap and then joined Chewbacca in the cockpit.

Finn hurried down the portside corridor, tapping the dome of R2-D2, the blue-and-white astromech who had also come on the mission. The droid decoupled from a recharging station and followed him.

A clank echoed from the *Falcon*'s hull. "We're docked!" Poe said over the ship's intercom.

Finn hit the control panel on the corridor wall. The

hatch above him opened. A scaly green face with two curved horns protruding from the skull and a smaller pair poking from the chin smiled down at him.

"Boolio, good to see you," Finn said. "You got something for us?"

"From a new ally—a spy in the First Order," the Ovissian said.

His statement hit Finn like a stunbolt. "A spy? Who?"

"I don't know. Transfer the message. Give it to Leia." Boolio dangled a cable through the portal. "Hurry!"

Finn took the cable and attached it to R2-D2's socket. "This could be big, Artoo."

The astromech chirped that he had a connection—and then proximity alarms rang throughout the ship. "Finn, we're about to be cooked!" Poe yelled.

Finn watched the droid's indicator lights. "Almost there!"

Right as R2-D2 tooted that the download was complete, Finn yanked out the cable and threw it back up to Boolio. "How do we thank you?"

"Win the war!" Boolio shouted, and then the hatch shut, sealing him off.

Enemy fire shook the *Falcon*. Finn snatched a tangle of wiring to steady himself. "You taking a break back there?" Poe said on the intercom. "We need a gunner!"

"On it!" Finn ran back through the lounge into the starboard corridor. A quick scramble down the access ladder and he was in the underside turret, strapping himself into the seat. The bubble-topped structures of the Sinta Glacier

Colony receded in the canopy, a view obstructed by a squadron of First Order TIE fighters.

Finn put on the headset and grabbed the twin firing grips. A group of flat-winged TIEs were hot on their tail as the *Falcon* raced through the frozen tunnels of a mega-comet. The TIEs unleashed their lasers, and one salvo struck the *Falcon*'s rear deflector, rocking the ship. Finn fired off a salvo of his own, blasting only ice from the tunnel wall.

Poe's voice popped in Finn's headset. "You're supposed to be getting rid of those things!"

In his former life as stormtrooper FN-2187, Finn had been trained in close quarters combat and ground warfare. Starship gunnery hadn't been in the curriculum. But if he didn't thin out the TIEs, not even Poe and Chewbacca's sensational piloting skills would save them.

He kept his eyes on the targeting computer and squared the TIE fighter in its sights. The second it acquired a lock, he pulled the trigger.

The *Falcon*'s lasers turned the TIE into a ball of flame. "Got one!" Finn hollered back.

"How many are left?" Poe asked.

"Too many," Finn said. He spun in the turret, tracking the closest TIE. It swerved right and left while the tunnel walls showed machinery embedded in the ice. They were nearing the giant drills the local mining company used to extract precious minerals from the comet.

Chewbacca barked something that seemed to improve

Poe's mood. "Good thinking, Chewie! Finn, we can boulder these TIEs!"

Finn flipped switches to divert more power to the cannons. "I was just thinking that."

The *Falcon* flipped on its axis and spun Finn upside down in the turret. He re-swallowed some of his breakfast rations and fired at the mining drill ahead. It wasn't a moving target, so his shots struck without a hitch. Chunks of machinery fell into the chasing TIEs, turning them into scrap.

Finn whooped. "Get us back to the base!" he said to Poe. He unbuckled from the gunner's seat and climbed up the ladder. Several moments later, he was in the cockpit standing next to Klaud, all his cheer gone.

Poe had them on a collision course with the ice wall of the megacomet.

Chewbacca howled, and Poe pulled a lever on the control board. The ice shattered before them into the straight lines of hyperspace.

The ship shuddered. Finn bounced into Klaud, Klaud bounced into Chewie, and Chewie kept howling while Poe kept his hand on the lever. Seconds later, the *Falcon* emerged in a colossal forest of translucent stalagmites, which Finn recognized from holo-adventures to be the legendary Crystal Chaos of Cardovyte. Some of the TIEs came out of lightspeed not far behind them.

Finn noticed Poe keying a new set of coordinates into the navicomputer. "What are you doing?"

"Lightspeed skipping." Poe pulled the lever again.

They jumped into a region of space packed with kilometer-high reflective spires that formed the architecture of the famous mirror city of Ivexia. Poe corkscrewed the *Falcon* around the buildings, dodging blasts from the TIEs that continued to pursue them.

Finn held on to the bulkhead. "How do you know how to do that?"

Chewbacca roared something about Rey. "Yeah, well, Rey's not here, is she?" Poe snapped back. He keyed more coordinates and pulled the lever a third time.

The navicomputer sent them to another wonder of the galaxy, an interstellar cloud of glowing green gases known as the Typhonic Nebula. There was no time to admire what few ever saw. Klaud cried out as the three-toothed maw of a giant space worm opened to ingest them.

"Last jump, maybe forever! Hold on!" Poe pulled the hyperspace lever again just before the *Falcon* would have been devoured. Finn knew the *Falcon*'s hyperdrive could blow at any time when put under such tremendous stress.

As the streaks of hyperspace filled the canopy, Klaud leaned his sensory antennae against Finn's shoulder. On impulse, Finn gave the Trodatome a comforting pat on the back as he would any squad mate. That hadn't been in the First Order's curriculum, either—but he did it anyway. It was the right thing to do.

CHAPTER 5

AFTER LEAVING EXEGOL, Kylo Ren didn't immediately return to his flagship. He jumped to Niful, a moon-sized asteroid in the Aniras belt. It had a thin, breathable atmosphere and a surface covered in sticky mud. He landed at the bottom of a crater and avoided any mud pits by climbing through a cleft in the crater wall. A passageway led him into a chamber of scalding, sweltering heat.

Albrekh the metalsmith, a long-eared, apelike Symeong, stoked the fires of a blast furnace. Surrounding him were six masked warriors in battered, mud-caked armor, brandishing crude and savage weaponry. Nearest to Ren was Vicrul, the self-proclaimed reaper of souls, who gained strength from every innocent life he harvested with his electro-scythe. Then there was Ushar, the interrogator of the bunch, skilled at using his war club to pound answers from prisoners. Kuruk served as the group's pilot and long-range sniper, while Cardo was their incinerator, equipped with a flamethrower cannon on his arm. The collector among them, Trudgen, liked to incorporate trophies of his victims in his gear, which included the visor of an Imperial death trooper and a Houk gladiator's vibrocleaver. Last, Ap'lek, a mastermind of traps and trickery, gripped a Mandalorian executioner's axe and wore a mask that was bent in a look of mock amusement.

These were the Knights of Ren, and the dark side clung to them like rot.

Kylo Ren glanced at them, not saying a word. Though masks covered any expression on their human and not-so-human faces, he sensed their bewilderment seeing their leader did not wear his.

Ren had smashed apart his mask in a fit of rage on the Mega-Destroyer, after Snoke had ridiculed him for wearing it and ordered him to take it off. But Ren had become so much more since then. He removed the pieces of the mask and helmet from a pouch on his belt and held them out. Hooting, Albrekh scampered over to grab them.

As the metalsmith went to work, Ren stood with the Knights, whose name he had taken from their former leader. These fearsome marauders, who fed on hate and death like rabid animals, prowled the remote spacelanes, plundering, killing, and sowing havoc wherever they went. Snoke had given the Knights to him as a reward, but it was he who had bested each in combat to become their leader. They stood with him, their bloodlust palpable, like they were grenades ready to explode.

The smith clamped the pieces of the helmet to his forge and poured liquid metal between the gaps. The metal was Sarrassian iron, found on asteroids in this belt. Ancient Sith alchemists had valued it in crafting weapons and armor, for it contained special particles that resonated with the dark side of the Force.

After being doused with water, the iron congealed, welding the helmet and mask together with dark red ribbons that resembled scars. Albrekh picked up the finished product with his smithy gloves and presented it to its owner.

The helmet felt sturdier than it had before, and Ren doubted he could smash it apart again. The mask also looked more intimidating. The visible red cracks split the silver bands around the eye slot and gashed the hinged mouth plate. He wondered what his grandfather would have thought of it. Vader had been required to don a mask, since his breathing depended on it. Ren, however, had a choice.

On Exegol, he had learned that the age-old enemies of the Jedi, the Sith, had not died out with Darth Vader. Their disciples kept the faith, waiting for someone like Ren to lead them.

As the Knights raised their weapons in salute, Kylo Ren put on his helmet. He would follow his grandfather's path and become the Dark Lord of the Sith.

CHAPTER 6

THE MIND OF A JEDI can move mountains. But the heart of the Jedi can move souls, wrote Master Lyr Farseeker. For there is more to the Jedi than the Force. There is kindness, there is compassion, there is light, and there is love.

She closed the book, a slim folio titled *Poetics of a Jedi*. She didn't want profound insights or riddles; what she needed was practical advice on interpreting visions. And since she had failed to communicate through the Force with Master Skywalker, her only hope for guidance seemed to lay in the texts she'd taken from Ahch-To.

There were eight leather-bound volumes in all, most handwritten in ink on a primitive material known as paper. They all had hard-to-pronounce titles. Chief among them was the *Rammahgon*, which was over five thousand years old and compiled the many origin stories of the Jedi. There were also two volumes of the *Aionomica*, which gathered philosophical writings about the Force. Her favorite of the eight was the *Chronicles of Brus-bu*, which she had consulted while trying to build her own lightsaber. She knew some chapters so well she could recite whole passages by memory.

The Jedi attune themselves to their saber's crystal, but the Sith attune the crystal to themselves. They corrupt and bleed it of power, as they do to everything they dominate. . . .

Luke had kept these books safe on Ahch-To, placing them inside the sacred tree. Before Rey had left Ahch-To, she had snuck into the tree and removed the entire library. She was a scavenger, after all, and the books had just been sitting there, collecting dust. They had seemed to call to her to take them.

She pulled the heavy *Rammahgon* from the shelf. The chapter she flipped to was authored by a Jedi named Kli the Elder. She started to read.

The Prime is One, but the Jedi are Many. The Sith were Many but often emerge Ruled by Two. The Seeds of the Jedi have been Sown throughout the Galaxy, on Ossus, Jedha, Xenxiar, and Others. The Sith have no Seeds, since what they Bury does not Grow. They are the Despoilers of Worlds, and have Laid to Waste once Fertile Habitats such as Korriban, Ziost, Ixigul, Asog, and Others.

She scanned through the rest of the chapter, but nothing jumped out as useful for contacting dead Jedi.

Nimi, a new human recruit who often cooked up delicious root stews for the base, rushed by the workbench. "Rey! *Falcon's* back!"

The news lifted Rey's spirits. She followed Nimi, BB-8, and a host of others out of the cave into the clearing. Rumors were circulating that the mission to Sinta had uncovered a spy in the First Order.

The *Millennium Falcon* always appeared to be one flight away from the junkyard. But as it landed, the freighter looked like it had already been there. Scorch marks discolored its exterior. Hull plates were gone. Conduits and wiring were exposed. Smoke spumed out from the engines, compressors, alternators, and even the landing gear.

"I need a fire crew, here! And another one in the back—go, go!" shouted Lieutenant Chireen, the quartermaster.

Poe was first down the *Falcon*'s ramp. "Hey," Rey called to him. "I heard there's a spy."

The dark-haired pilot halted before her. "We could've really used you out there." Ever since she had worked with him and Rose to stop the First Order on Minfar, he had wanted her out in the field as much as possible.

Rey avoided commenting on what had been Leia's decision for her to stay and train. "How'd it go?" she asked.

"Really bad, actually. Really bad." Poe turned to BB-8, who had rolled up to him and cheeped. The droid still was missing a panel on his body after it was knocked loose when the tree fell on him. "What'd you do to the droid?"

"What'd you do to the *Falcon*?" Rey countered.

"The *Falcon*'s in a lot better shape than he is."

"Beebee-Ate's not on fire—"

"What's left of him isn't on fire," Poe retorted.

Rey tried to keep her cool. "Tell me what happened."

"You tell me first," Poe demanded.

BB-8 rotated his dome back and forth between them. Rey narrowed her eyes at Poe. "You know what you are?"

"What?"

"You're difficult. Really difficult," she said. "You're a difficult man."

"And you are—"

"Finn!" Rey spotted her best friend coming down the *Falcon*'s ramp. She hurried toward him and gave him a hug. "You made it back!"

"Barely." In the months since Crait, he'd grown out his hair longer than stormtrooper regulation and had cut off the sleeves of a brand-new flight jacket he had picked out for himself. But his smile was as big as it had been on the day she'd first met him.

She could hear BB-8 telling Poe about the incident with the tree but ignored them. "Do we have a spy?" she asked Finn.

Before Finn could reply, Chewbacca emerged from the hatch, grumbling about the *Falcon*. She spun back to Poe. "You lightspeed-skipped?"

"It got us back here, didn't it?" he said.

"Poe, the compressor's down—"

"I know, I was there," he shot back.

"You can't lightspeed-skip the *Falcon*!" Rey insisted.

Poe stood up from his crouch beside BB-8. "Actually, it turns out you can," he said, and started to walk away from her.

"Hey, both of you, we just landed, okay?" Finn said.

Rey wasn't listening. This was the *Millennium Falcon*

they were talking about, the legendary ship that made the Kessel Run in less than twelve parsecs, and Poe was treating it like a flight-test vessel.

She went after Poe, wanting an explanation. "What happened?"

"Bad news, is what happened," Poe said.

Rey became even angrier. Fighter pilots could be so uncooperative. "Did we make contact with the spy or not?"

Walking beside her, Finn answered the question. "There's a mole in the First Order. They sent us a message."

Poe turned on Rey, clearly as exasperated as she was. "You dropped a tree on him," he said, indicating BB-8.

"You blew *both* sub-alternators," she said.

Finn stepped between them. "Guys—"

Poe kept arguing with Rey. "Well, maybe you should be out there with us."

"You know I want to be," she said.

"But you're not. You're here training, for what?" Poe's tone softened, ever so slightly. "You're the best fighter we have. We need you out *there*, not *here*." He strode off, waving down a young Mon Calamari officer in a beige jumpsuit. "Junior! Get Artoo's data transferred and into reconditioning."

Glowering, Rey looked at Finn for support. But he took Poe's side. "It's true."

Rey let out a breath. Their criticism stung, perhaps because they had a point. But she didn't want to talk about it anymore. "What's the message?"

"'I send this as a warning to the Resistance,'" the protocol droid C-3PO said, while decoding the spy's message. "'Emperor Palpatine somehow cheated death.'"

Like everyone gathered in the command center, Finn had heard the Emperor's broadcast declaring his triumphant return. Many in the Resistance had doubted the transmission's authenticity, surmising it was a First Order scheme to scare rebellious systems. But this message, from a spy within the First Order, seemed to quash those doubts.

"Are we sure we can believe this?" asked Commander Tico, or as Finn knew her, Rose. After Rose's heroics on Crait, General Organa had promoted the young maintenance tech to head the Resistance Engineering Corps.

"It cannot be. The Emperor is dead," said the Mon Calamari who had assisted Poe. Affectionately called Junior around the base, the bulbous-eyed officer was Aftab Ackbar, son of the legendary Admiral Ackbar, who had perished on the *Raddus*. "He was killed aboard the second Death Star."

Beaumont Kin, a short, bearded man who had been a professor before joining the Resistance, offered an explanation. "There are historical accounts of techniques that were meant to subvert physical death. Dark science . . . cloning. Secrets only the Sith knew."

The mere mention of the Sith sent a chill down Finn's spine. The Sith were supposed to be extinct, like their enemies, the Jedi. But that was his stormtrooper training talking. Ever since he'd left the First Order, he had discovered most of what he'd been taught was a lie. Luke Skywalker was real, the Jedi were real, the Force was real, which meant, as much as he didn't want to admit it, the Sith had to be real.

"So the Emperor did die," Poe said, "but something came back."

The general's personal adviser, the short-haired, whip-smart Commander D'Acy, weighed in with a frightful speculation. "He must have been behind the First Order. It was Palpatine all along."

If what D'Acy said was true, had Finn and all his storm-trooper squad mates been trained to become pawns of the Emperor? Finn shuddered at the thought.

At last General Organa spoke. "Always, in the shadows, this man. From the very beginning."

Her words left the crowd numb. But Finn suspected that Boolio wouldn't have risked his life just to confirm the Emperor's return. "Is that it, Threepio?"

"I wish it were, sir, but . . ." The gold-plated droid conveyed more of the spy's message. "'He's been found by Kylo Ren. Now the two are on the verge of'—oh my!"

"What?" Poe demanded.

C-3PO sounded distraught as he continued. "'The two are on the verge of deploying a fleet unlike any the galaxy has ever seen.'"

Dread descended on the group like a cloud. An additional fleet would make the First Order unstoppable.

Aftab wrung his webbed hands. "They'll crush us! My father warned this day would come."

Beaumont Kin nodded. "We're not ready. Only half our ships are working. We have no large-scale weapons."

"So we fix them," Rose Tico piped in, "fast."

"I'm afraid the news gets worse," C-3PO said. "The message says that there is little time left. Somehow the Resistance must find Exegol, the hidden world of the Sith—and launch a surprise attack while there is still hope."

Finn noticed that Rey furrowed her brow when C-3PO identified the world. Did she know of it?

"Never heard of Exegol," said Major Wexley, nicknamed Snap for his nervous habit of snapping his fingers.

Lieutenant Connix did a quick check on her datapad. "It's not on our star charts."

"It's not on any star chart," said Maz Kanata. The orange-skinned ex-pirate had been a sworn enemy of the First Order since its TIE fighters had destroyed her castle on Takodana. She'd joined the Resistance recently and served as an informal adviser to Leia.

"Exegol is hidden, a world kept secret by generations of Sith Lords," Maz said. "It lies deep in the Unknown Regions, the darkest place there is."

Snap grumbled, "How can we attack a place we can't find?"

General Organa remained composed and collected, as always. "Friends, this is the moment that counts. Everything we've fought for is at stake."

Beaumont Kin brought home the general's words. "If this fleet launches, freedom dies in the galaxy."

The preparations for the mission began immediately, but Finn did not join in as he normally would have. He saw Rey slip out of the command center, so he followed.

Exegol.

The planet's name struck a chord with Rey. She recalled seeing it somewhere in the Jedi texts.

She sat down on the chair in her workshop and skimmed millennia of scholarship in a matter of minutes. When she was finished with one book, she took another. Her task might have been easier with R2-D2, but he was involved in the mission planning. The droid had imaged the contents of all the volumes and could have performed a quick sort-and-search routine on the text. Then again, he might not have been able to find a match. Many of the writings were in long-dead languages, and R2-D2 did not have the translation capabilities his counterpart, C-3PO, possessed.

Fortunately, Rey had translated parts of the texts herself with the help of C-3PO and the base's resident history professor, Beaumont Kin. Those translations gave her a strong foundation concerning what each book contained.

"Exegol, Exegol," she said to herself as she scanned the chapters of the *Rammahgon*. She was reading so fast she nearly missed it.

The Sith have no Seeds, since what they Bury does not

*Grow. They are the Despoilers of Worlds, and have Laid to
Waste once Fertile Habitats such as Korriban, Ziost, Ixigul—*

There it was. Ixigul. It had to be an alternate spelling of
Exegol. And in the margin of the same page Luke Skywalker
had made annotations in a secret code.

A cough behind her made her turn in her seat. Finn
stood beside her tool caddy. "How long have you been
there?" she asked.

"About as long as you've been in here," he said.

"I didn't even know," Rey said. She'd been so absorbed
in her reading. "But look, I found a clue to the planet."

"Exegol?"

She gestured Finn over to the bench. "The Jedi had
been trying to find it for a generation. Luke Skywalker was
searching for it with an ally, but the trail went cold."

"Who was the ally?"

Rey glanced again at the page. "He doesn't say."

Finn leaned over her shoulder for a look at the book.
"What else does it say?"

Rey traced her finger over Luke's annotations as she
spoke. "Luke sensed a great evil rising in the galaxy. He
made an appeal to the Jedi that came after, to take up the
search"—she paused as she figured out the last line—"and
bring an end to the galaxy's evil once and for all."

Finn took in what she'd said, then looked at her. "The
Jedi that came after? Rey . . . he's talking to you."

Rey blinked. Finn was implying that she should be the
one to take up the search for Exegol. But after her visions

and her failure in the jungle, going to the hidden world of the Sith seemed like a dangerous proposition. On such a world, the dark side would tempt her with all it had to offer—and she worried she might fall for its bait.

"That's not a good idea," she said.

Finn regarded her with skepticism. "What's all your training, if not for this?" he asked. "Poe's right, you need to be out there, in the fight. Continue Luke's search."

"Finn, I can't—"

"Why not?"

"Ren," she said. There was truth to that. Kylo Ren was hunting her, and he would keep hunting her until she turned to the dark side—his side.

"I'll protect you," Finn said.

Rey would have found those words condescending if they came out of anyone else's mouth. But Finn's concern for her was sincere. She smiled and put her hand on his cheek. "Even you can't do that," she said. The simple fact was that against Kylo Ren, the Emperor, or any Sith for that matter, Finn would be the one who needed protection.

Finn looked back at her and for once didn't argue.

CHAPTER 7

THERE WAS A WEAPON more powerful than Death Stars or Dreadnoughts—more powerful than even the Starkiller. It didn't have a trigger. It didn't shoot a blast. It couldn't even kill. Yet it could cause the most courageous of soldiers to quake in their boots and could compel masses of beings to do one's bidding.

That weapon was fear.

Kylo Ren strode down the corridors of the Star Destroyer *Steadfast*, which served as his flagship after the Resistance had damaged the *Finalizer* at the Battle of Batuu. The Knights of Ren stomped behind him. Along the corridor, First Order officers snapped to attention. Stormtroopers raised their hands in salute. Ren commanded their respect not only because he was their Supreme Leader but because they feared him. Fear kept them in line. Fear made them serve him.

The flagship's commander, Admiral Griss, waited for Ren with his staff near the detention area. Ren halted, as did the Knights.

"Supreme Leader." Griss saluted Ren and then motioned

to a group of stormtroopers. They pushed forward a roughed-up Ovissian. Green blood dripped from still fresh wounds on his chin and arms. Three of his four horns were cracked.

"This is the one called Boolio," Griss said. "Captured at the Sinta Glacier Colony, sir—a traitor."

Ren knew they expected him to interrogate this prisoner, as he had done with so many others. But the time for questions was over. He lit his saber.

Boolio looked Ren straight in the mask, without a hint of fear. One swift downward arc put an end to his defiance.

The troopers moved in to take the body. Ren grabbed the decapitated head. He gestured for the Knights to remain with the admiral while he strode toward a lift.

A meeting of the Supreme Council was in progress when Ren marched into the conference room and planted the Ovissian's head on the table. "We have a spy in our ranks who just sent a message to the Resistance," Ren said, his mask's vocoder clipping his voice.

The men and women at the table sat up with a start. Ren circled the table, taking note of each council member. One of them had leaked information about his discoveries on Exegol. Only Allegiant General Pryde's loyalty did he not question. Having served in the Imperial military, Pryde had spent his career championing the Empire's authoritarian methods of domination and oppression. He believed in the First Order's supremacy with a religious zeal.

Ren was less sure about the others. General Quinn was a hot-tempered cynic whose vocal distrust of Ren made him a suspect. Also in attendance were chief strategist General Parnadee, intelligence officer Kandia, Commander Trach, and General Engell, whom Ren had put in charge of the stormtrooper legions after Captain Phasma's demise.

And of course there was General Armitage Hux, an arrogant man with an arrogant face. Hux had believed that Supreme Leader Snoke was grooming him to take over the First Order, until Ren had disposed of Snoke and assumed the mantle of command for himself. But Hux had been born and bred into the First Order and was as firm a supporter of it as Pryde was. He'd die before betraying it.

"Whoever this traitor is, it won't stop us." Ren went to the viewport and looked out at the universe he would control. "With what I've seen on Exegol, the First Order is about to become a true empire."

He turned to consider the youngest of the generals. "I sense unease about my appearance, General Hux."

Most members of the council shifted to look at Hux. "About the mask?" Hux asked, doing his best to project confidence. "No, sir. Well done."

Seated next to Hux, General Engell made sure to offer a compliment of her own. "I like it."

"Forgive me, sir," said General Quinn. "But these allies on Exegol sound like a cult. Conjurers and soothsayers."

"They've conjured legions of Star Destroyers," Pryde said. "The Sith fleet will increase our resources ten thousandfold. Such range and power will correct the error of Starkiller Base." He looked at Hux, making it clear where he thought the blame for the destruction of Starkiller Base lay.

General Parnadee went right into logistics. "We'll need to increase recruitments, harvest more of the galaxy's young—"

"First," Ren said, "I need the scavenger."

"Respectfully, sir, but your preoccupation with the girl is maddening," General Quinn said. "We have more pressing issues. This fleet, what is it, a gift? What is he asking for in return? Does that mean—"

Ren stretched out a hand. The general flew out of his chair and slammed into the ceiling. Hovering there, he gasped as his body shook back and forth. The others frowned, yet no one spoke up in defense of Quinn. They just watched him being throttled.

"Prepare to crush any worlds that defy us," Ren said. "My Knights and I are going hunting for the scavenger."

He lowered his hand. General Quinn dropped onto the table, dead. Whether he had been the one to contact the rebels or not, Ren doubted there would be any more leaks.

Though Rey wasn't going on the search for Exegol, she wanted to provide the Resistance with all the information she could. She enlisted the help of Beaumont Kin, and the two read through Luke's notes and the corresponding text in the *Rammahgon*. BB-8 joined them in her workshop for moral support. The droid looked as good as new, having had all his dents banged out and his panel replaced.

"My conclusion is you cannot go to Exegol unless you have one of *these*," Kin said. He flipped to a page in the book and showed them illustrations of objects shaped like pyramids. "Sith wayfinders. Ancient things. There were always two. One for the Sith master, one for the apprentice."

Rey stared at the drawings. She had seen them before in her studies. She had assumed they had something to do with the Force and the Jedi, not the Sith.

"Luke was on the hunt for the Emperor's wayfinder." Kin pointed at the largest of the pyramidal sketches. "But his trail went cold on a desert world called Pasaana."

"In the Middian system?"

"You been? Can't get a decent meal there," Kin said.

"So Leia will start the search on Pasaana," Rey said.

"*You* will start the search on Pasaana," said Maz Kanata, sauntering into Rey's workshop.

Beaumont Kin let out a yawn that Rey knew was fake and excused himself. Maz shuffled closer to Rey's chair. "Leia will stay behind to plan the attack on the fleet," Maz said. "But there can be no attack until you've completed Luke's mission to find Exegol."

"Maz, if Leia sends me, I'll be a danger to the mission—to everyone. Someone else has to go."

"There is no one else. The search for Exegol is a task for the Jedi."

Rey slid off her chair. "I'm not a Jedi. Not yet—I'm not ready. I'm not as strong as Leia thinks."

"You won't know how strong you are until you know how

strong you have to be." Maz could be so baffling with her riddles.

"The dark side has plans for me," Rey said. "If I go, Kylo Ren will find me."

"You have faced him before," Maz said.

"It's not him I'm afraid of," Rey said.

Maz plopped her goggles over her eyes, as if trying to see more of Rey. After a long look, she offered up another riddle. "To find the darkest place in the galaxy, you will need to face the darkest part of yourself," she said. "You must go. The Force has led you here. You must trust in it. Always."

Rey pondered what the pirate-philosopher said long after Maz had left. She knew she would regret it if she didn't search for the wayfinder. But she would do it by herself.

She gathered a few belongings from her workshop and walked out of the cave into the clearing where the *Millennium Falcon* was parked. The freighter might have sustained some damage from Poe's reckless flying, but Rey wouldn't take any other ship. A few quick patches to the compressors would make it spaceworthy again.

Rey was disconnecting a hose on the ignition line when Poe Dameron approached. "You were right before," she said. "I can't stay here to train while others do all the fighting. I'm going to pick up Luke's search for Exegol. I'm going to start where the trail went cold, on the desert world of—"

"We know," Poe interrupted. "We're going with you."

He didn't even let her argue otherwise. He ducked under the *Falcon*'s forward mandible while Finn walked over.

Rey shook her head. "I need to do this alone."

"Alone with your friends," Finn said.

"No," she said, "it's too dangerous."

But Finn would not back down. "That's why we go *together*," he said.

Poe returned with Chewbacca and BB-8. The Wookiee ruffed that she wasn't flying the *Falcon* without him—Han wouldn't have allowed it.

Rey smiled at his joke. It was good to have friends.

Leia was in pain.

By all accounts, she should be dead. The First Order's attack on the cruiser *Raddus* should've killed her, as it had Admiral Ackbar and many other Resistance commanders on the ship's bridge. But when Leia had been floating among the debris in the cold of space, she'd realized that her duties were not done. So she sank into the Force to cocoon her body and sustain her life until she had drifted back into an undamaged section of the *Raddus*. Resistance medics did the rest, and she was able to recover in a matter of days. One of the droids, a 2-1B model who had served Leia since the Alliance, proclaimed that her survival defied all logic. It was, in words surprising for a droid, a miracle.

Leia's entire life felt like a miracle, she readily admitted. Perseverance and luck played a big part in her survival, but she would never discount the impact of the Force. Whether she was conscious of it or not, the Force had guided her in times of crisis. It had also helped her heal her body.

But it had not healed her heart.

Alone in her quarters in a corner of the cave, she retrieved a memento from a flight case. Flower petals representing the Old Republic were engraved on a gold medal with a rising sun symbolizing the Rebel Alliance at its center. It was the Alliance's Medal of Bravery, awarded to a select few for acts of courage. Her husband, Han Solo, had earned it during the Battle of Yavin.

Though it had been decades, she remembered the day she had decorated him with the medal. After she had given it to him, he had winked at her, as if he knew their story had just begun. She, on the other hand, had pursed her lips and kept her poise. A military ceremony was no place to flirt. And who did he think he was? A scoundrel like Han Solo would never get a princess like her, not in a million years.

And yet he had. And they'd had a son. And that son had made her a widow.

"When you gave Han that medal, how could you know where your life would take you?" croaked a voice. Leia turned to see Maz Kanata in the entrance to her quarters. The pirate shared Leia's sensitivity to the Force, so Leia was not surprised that Maz could discern her feelings.

"I know you fear Rey's pull to the dark side," Maz said, "that you had visions of her death. But as you have often reminded me, the future is uncertain. The girl must find her true path."

"True path," Leia murmured. She had told Maz about

the nightmares she had, in which she saw this brilliant girl she had taken under her wing follow her son's path into the darkness. And the darkness would be too much. It would suffocate Rey. It would destroy her, as it had Ben.

Yet Rey was not Ben.

Leia thought about the time when she herself was young and impetuous, a teenager elected to represent Alderaan in the Imperial Senate. She had risked her own life, and those of the crew of the *Tantive IV*, to transport stolen data-tapes containing the readouts to the Death Star. She had looked into the face of darkness itself—the mask of Darth Vader—and endured the agony of his torture, yet had not surrendered the location of the rebel base.

Was what Rey planned to do any more foolish? Feisty, headstrong, and stubborn to the bone—the girl from Jakku reminded Leia of herself.

Maz stepped closer to Leia: "Your spirit is strong, my friend. But you are not well. Your body grows weaker. Give her your blessing. Give her Luke's saber." The lightsaber hilt lay on Leia's desk, where she had placed it after Rey had handed it to her. Maz picked it up and presented it to Leia. "While you still can. While there is still hope."

Leia peered at the pirate and the saber she held. Maz had seen many things over her long life, and the fact that she had joined the Resistance meant that she thought its fight against the First Order was of utmost necessity.

When Leia went to the mouth of the cave, she overheard C-3PO saying farewell to R2-D2. "In the event I do not return, I want you to know you have been a real friend, Artoo. My best one, in fact."

Leia smiled. Never underestimate a droid's capacity for tenderness. She had authorized C-3PO to go with Rey, knowing they could use his services as an interpreter and a diplomat. But he was more than his programming, as was R2-D2. The fight for freedom she had waged her entire life had not just been for organic beings but all those who could be caring and compassionate, including droids.

Her student stood near the *Falcon*, talking to Poe. "Rey?" Leia called.

Their eyes met. Rey walked up to her, appearing apologetic. "There's so much I want to tell you," she said.

"Tell me when you get back," Leia said, and held out Luke's lightsaber.

Rey stared at the hilt, as if unsure whether to take it. Leia continued to offer it with a gentle smile. After a moment, Rey took the lightsaber from her and then embraced Leia.

Leia whispered into the girl's ear. "Never be afraid of who you are."

Rey looked at Leia and nodded.

As the *Millennium Falcon*'s engines warmed for launch, Maz came to stand next to Leia. "If she finds Exegol, she may just survive. But if she doesn't"—Maz, who was always sure of herself, hesitated—"the galaxy surely will not."

Leia watched the *Falcon* soar above the treetops. Despite giving Rey the saber, she worried about the girl like she still worried about her son. A mother's worries.

CHAPTER 8

REY SCANNED the Pasaana desert with quadnoculars. There was nothing but mountains and rocks and dunes and sand.

It reminded her of home.

Before meeting BB-8 and Finn, she had roamed such desolate stretches on Jakku for hours, sometimes even days, alone. Always alone. Lost in her own thoughts. Scavenging for whatever might be of worth. Rarely ever seeing another form of life. And when she did trade in the scrap she'd found, she didn't stay long at Niima Outpost to socialize, unless an off-worlder had a good story to tell. Mostly she went back to her abandoned Imperial walker, to be by herself. She spent those cold and quiet nights researching old legends, practicing her piloting skills on a simulator, or gazing at the stars and thinking of her parents. She pined for the day they would return and take her away to somewhere pleasant, somewhere she could truly call home.

She'd never really thought of Jakku as her home until she had left it.

"We sure we landed in the right place?" Poe stood on an

outcropping beside her and Finn. He wore a scarf around his neck to protect him against the sand and wind. Chewbacca and the droids came up from the *Falcon* behind them.

"These are the exact coordinates Master Luke left behind," C-3PO stated, though no one had asked him.

Something boomed in the distance, followed by what sounded like loud crooning. "What was that?" Poe asked.

C-3PO eagerly offered his expertise. "It sounds like the end of a local Aki-Aki prayer—"

Finn put up his hand. "Shhh, Threeps!"

The noise repeated: *boom-boom-boom*. Rey suspected it was the beating of a drum, in harmony with a chorus of voices, all chanting in unison.

She took the group in the direction of the sound. Rounding a rocky butte, she stopped in astonishment. Down in the valley, thousands of the planet's native population, the Aki-Aki, had gathered to dance, sing, and play instruments around bonfires. A couple of treadables—the split-track landcrawlers the Aki-Aki drove across the desert wastes—deposited even more celebrants.

"Why, it is!" C-3PO waggled his arms excitedly. "We happen to have arrived the very day of their Festival of the Ancestors, which happens once every forty-two years!"

"Well, that's lucky," Finn snorted.

"Lucky indeed!" C-3PO exclaimed. "The festival is meant to be delightful! It's known for its colorful kites and delectable sweets."

Rey, Poe, and Finn stared at him. For C-3PO, it was as if sightseeing and saving the galaxy were one and the same.

Once they waded into the crowds, Rey had to admit the festival *was* delightful. Using their prehensile trunks like an extra pair of hands, Aki-Aki musicians pounded drums, blew pipes, and banged cymbals to produce an entrancing melody. Colored smoke swirled around dancers in equally colorful robes, who swung their double trunks in rhythm to the beat. Others tended the bonfires or sold water orbs and sweetmallow candies to those who watched the dance. A fair number of outsiders mingled about to witness the spectacular cultural event for themselves.

"I've never seen anything like it," Rey said.

"I've never seen so few wayfinders," Finn retorted.

Poe looked around warily. "There's always random First Order patrols in crowds like these. So keep your heads down . . . especially you, Chewie."

While Poe, Finn, and Chewbacca continued farther into the festival, with the Wookiee ducking his head, Rey hung back with C-3PO and BB-8. A puppeteer performed a rendition of an Aki-Aki myth with dolls dangling on strings, but Rey was more fascinated by the children who watched the show. The small Aki-Aki giggled and cooed, crawling around on the ground or bounding about on stumpy feet. Having not yet grown their double trunks, they looked like bundles of baby fat, clapping doughy hands in glee and blinking button-sized eyes.

An Aki-Aki girl in a green robe pulled on Rey's capelet. Rey knelt down to the little girl and received a gift for doing so. The girl placed a necklace made from kern-nut husks around Rey's collar. Rey smiled in appreciation. "Thank you."

BB-8 rolled around the girl and chirped. "My friend's asking what the fires are for," Rey said.

The girl responded in the Aki-Aki language. C-3PO translated. "Their ancestors live in the fire. This is how they show their gratitude. She says her name is Nambi Ghima."

"That's an excellent name. I'm Rey."

Nambi tooted a question. "She would be honored to know your family name, too," C-3PO said.

Rey nearly winced. "I don't have one. I'm just Rey."

As she said her name again, she felt a presence tug at her mind. She stood and walked away from the puppet show. The music and chanting went quiet, and the bonfires roared as darkness descended around her. She knew immediately this wasn't a vision. This was a connection she had to someone she despised. A bond through the Force.

In the darkness she perceived Kylo Ren, wearing his old mask, which was dented and cracked like the young man who wore it. "Palpatine wants you dead."

"Serving another master?" she snapped back at him.

"No, I have other plans," he said. "I offered you my hand once. You wanted to take it. Why didn't you?"

"You could have killed me. Why didn't you?"

"You can't hide, Rey. Not from me."

"I see through the cracks in your mask," she said. "You're haunted. You can't stop seeing what you did to your father."

"Do you still count the days since your parents left?"

She expected he would say something like that to goad her, provoke her anger. And in the past it might have worked. But she was stronger since they'd last clashed. Leia had taught her much.

"Such pain in you. Such anger." He seemed to come closer to her. "I don't want to have to kill you. I'm going to find you and turn you to the dark side. When I offer you my hand again, you'll take it."

"We'll see," she said.

Ren's black-gloved hand reached toward her and grabbed the necklace, tearing it off her. And then his presence vanished from her mind and she was back at the festival, in the daylight.

She gasped and felt her bare neck. The necklace was gone. By some trick of the Force, he had taken it from her. And if he had it, he would analyze its beads and know she was on Pasaana.

She motioned C-3PO and BB-8 to come with her as she hustled through the crowds, leading with her staff. She found Finn, Chewbacca, and Poe making inquiries with a merchant.

"We have to go back to the *Falcon*," she said between breaths. "It's Ren. He knows we're here." She started heading out of the festival grounds without further explanation. The others joined her, with C-3PO trying to keep up.

A First Order stormtrooper spied them rounding a tent. "Freeze, right there!" He aimed his rifle at them and clicked his comm to alert his squad. "I've located the Resistance fugitives—"

A metal bolt plunged into the trooper's visor. The trooper collapsed and his comlink went silent. A figure in brown robes and a saucer-shaped helmet emerged from the tent carrying a prod pistol. "Follow me—hurry!" the figure said through a mask.

The rescuer headed in the opposite direction of where Rey had been going. Rey gave the others a nod and they all went after the figure. C-3PO struggled to stay with them. "Oh, slow down! What sort of friends are you?"

The masked figure moved through the crowds, arriving at one of the giant treadables. Two grip tracks encased the vehicle's huge wheels, allowing it to roll over rocky terrain. It was already moving, and the figure leapt into its cargo cage. Rey and her group did the same, with Chewbacca pulling C-3PO into the treadable with him.

"Leia sent me a transmission. Told me you might need a helping hand," the figure said, then parted a bead curtain to give directions to the driver. "To the east passage, Kalo'ne!"

Trinkets and wares from all over Pasaana filled the cargo compartment, dangling from the ceiling and walls, all for sale. Rey, however, was more interested in this masked figure and why he or she had rescued them.

Finn voiced her question. "There are thousands out there. How'd you find us?"

The figure pulled off the helmet, revealing a dark-haired human with a gray mustache and a smile that could charm an Ugnaught. "Wookiees stand out in a crowd."

Chewbacca roared with joy and pushed Finn aside to embrace the man. "Good to see you, too, old buddy!" his friend said, trying not to be smothered.

C-3PO perked up from almost having been left behind. "This is General Lando Calrissian. Allow me to give you a complete history of—"

"We know who he is, Threepio," Rey said. Lando was one of the greatest heroes of the Rebellion, the gambler turned general who had helmed the *Falcon* in the successful attack on the Empire's second Death Star. He also had been a close friend of Han and Leia's.

Finn shared her excitement. "It is an honor, General."

Poe cut to the chase. "General Calrissian, we're looking for Exegol."

Lando took them all in for a moment. "Of course you are." He touched his wrist comlink. It projected a hologram of a pyramidal object with strange markings.

"A Sith wayfinder," Rey said. "Luke Skywalker came here to find one."

Lando chuckled. "I know, I was with him. Luke and I were tailing an old Jedi hunter, Ochi of Bestoon." Lando hit another button on his comlink. The holo shifted into what appeared to be a black-eyed humanoid wearing a cybernetic implant around the back of his head. "Ochi had bragged he knew where the wayfinder was, locked in a vault somewhere.

He had a clue to its location inscribed on something he was carrying. We followed his ship halfway across the galaxy to Pasaana. When we got here, his ship was abandoned. No Ochi, no clue, and no wayfinder."

"So you stayed here?" Finn asked.

"For a time. The desert helps you forget." Lando grew serious. "The First Order went after us, the leaders from the old wars. They took our kids, turned them into our enemies. Han and Leia's son, Ben. My girl. She wasn't even old enough to walk. Far as I know, she's a stormtrooper now. They wanted to kill the spirit of the Rebellion for good."

"We're sorry to hear that, General. But our mission might stop the First Order from doing such things in the future." Rey paused, out of respect for what he had said. "Do you know if Ochi's ship is still here?"

Lando turned off his comlink. The hologram fizzled away. "It's out in the desert, where he left it."

"We need to get to that ship, search it," Rey said. Poe nodded in agreement.

High-pitched engines whined outside the treadable. Rey peeked out an opening in the compartment, though she didn't need to. She knew that sound by heart—TIE fighters.

"I've got a bad feeling about this," Lando said. "Ochi's ship is out past Lurch Canyon. Go."

Chewbacca ruffed a heartfelt farewell before he jumped out of the treadable. "You too, Chewie," Lando said.

The others went after the Wookiee. Rey was last and looked back at Lando. "Leia needs pilots, General."

That made Lando grin again. "My flying days are long gone. But do me a favor. Give Leia my love."

Lando's smile could melt hearts, but Rey sensed that pain and loneliness lurked underneath. She braved a suggestion. "You should give it to her yourself. Thank you."

His smile wavered, the slightest twitch. And then he was out of her sight as Rey leapt out of the treadable.

She landed on both feet in the sand. "There! Those speeders!" Poe yelled, leading the group into a parking area for the festival. He hot-wired two open-air skimmers in no time.

C-3PO arrived just as some of the locals took notice of them. "No need to worry. I made it!"

Rey, BB-8, and Chewbacca hopped aboard the smaller of the two craft, an old cargo transport, while Poe, C-3PO, and Finn climbed onto a newer-model loader. Both contained bundles of farm produce ostensibly to be sold at the festival market. Poe gunned his skimmer's engines and Rey followed. She wished they hadn't needed to steal the vehicles, but what they were doing was for the good of the galaxy and the Aki-Aki.

They sped through the badlands, the two skimmers side by side. Holding the tiller, Rey relished the wind whipping dust and sand in her face. For the second time that day, she felt at home, as if she were on Jakku riding her junkspeeder back from a scavenging expedition. BB-8 turned his dome toward her and beeped loudly.

"It doesn't go any faster, BB-8!" Rey had locked the repulsorlift engines to maximum acceleration.

In the skimmer next to her, she could hear Finn shout at Poe. "Ripping speeders, lightspeed-skipping—how do you know how to do shifty stuff like that?"

Poe shrugged. "Just stuff I picked up."

"Where?" Finn asked.

A hail of laserfire splattered food sacks in the rear of Poe and Finn's skimmer. Rey glanced back and saw why BB-8 had been skittish. Two First Order treadspeeders—track-geared patrol bikes that grappled the rough surface—ripped through the sands after them, each carrying a pair of stormtroopers.

Rey and Poe tilted their skimmers to dodge the treadspeeders' lasers. Finn drew his blaster, Chewbacca his bowcaster. Both returned fire. The speeders' drivers shifted their forward treads to the side, pluming up dust. Their passengers, meanwhile, launched off the treadspeeders with rocket packs.

"Oh, we're done for!" C-3PO cried. "They fly now!"

"They fly now?" Finn said.

"They fly now!" Poe screamed into the wind. "Rey! We should split—"

"Up!" Rey said, having the same idea.

Poe directed his skimmer toward a canyon. Rey turned hers toward a dustgrain farm. The treadspeeders also diverged to follow, though both jet troopers flew after Rey.

Chewbacca shot bowcaster rounds at the pursuing vehicle. The treadspeeder pivoted on its rotating track and eluded the plasma quarrels. Hovering over them, the jet troopers fired timed charges into the sand in front of the skimmer. Rey banked the skimmer on its side to avoid an exploding charge, then righted it to dodge a second explosion.

"Get them!" Rey yelled to Chewie. "I'll go for the speeder!"

The Wookiee aimed up at the jet troopers, causing them to move farther apart. With one hand on the tiller, Rey drew her blaster pistol and shot at the treadspeeder. A deflector field around the vehicle shimmered, absorbing her shots.

"Their front shields are up!" Rey said.

BB-8 started blabbering about a canister in the skimmer. "Not now!" Rey said, trying to steer and aim at the same time.

Chewbacca barked and pointed a long arm. On a bluff ahead of them lay the outline of a starship, which had to be Ochi's vessel. "I see it!" Rey said.

She couldn't take a longer look at it because lasers hammered the skimmer's deck. She yanked the tiller to dodge another blast. A jet trooper plummeted from the sky into the sand, struck by Chewbacca's quarrel. The Wookiee bellowed in triumph and took aim at the other trooper.

Rey brought the skimmer into a field of electro-sifter poles that resembled moisture vaporators on Jakku. The remaining jet trooper soared past them, dropping explosive charges. Behind them, the treadspeeder was gaining, its lasers getting too close for Rey's comfort. Rey had to steer through both the sifters and a minefield of charges while shooting back at the treadspeeder. But her blaster bolts were too weak to penetrate the speeder's shields.

BB-8 extended his welding arm and sliced open the canister just before the skimmer swerved. The canister tumbled off the side and took flight, propelled by the pressurized gases it emitted. It exploded in a yellowish cloud that matched the smoke used at the festival.

The cloud was so thick it completely engulfed the treadspeeder. Blinded, the driver never saw the boulder in his path. The treadspeeder struck it and launched into the air. Rey got off a shot at the speeder's underbelly repulsors that caused it to explode.

"Never underestimate a droid!" Rey said to BB-8's yips.

The jet trooper had flown too far away for Chewbacca to target, so for the moment they weren't being harassed. Rey navigated the skimmer through the last stretch of the dust-grain farm. She could see the starship parked on a butte on the desert flats beyond. It was an older transport model she couldn't identify, yet it looked eerily familiar. Two cylindrical engines buttressed a trapezoidal fuselage.

"Ochi's ship," she said to Chewbacca, squinting at it. "I've seen it before somewhere."

Poe sped his skimmer out of Lurch Canyon and caught up with hers. A piece of a treadspeeder part bounced behind them, wound in a rope tied to the skimmer's mast. They must have used a grappling hook to stop their pursuer.

"You get all of 'em?" Poe shouted.

Rey scanned the sky. "There's one left."

The jet trooper rocketed over Ochi's starship and came at them, unloading projectiles. Charges landed on both speeders and detonated, tossing everyone off. The impact of their landing was soft enough that Rey and Chewbacca managed to roll onto a knee and shoot. The Wookiee's quarrel nailed the trooper in the pack while Rey burned a hole in his armor. Whirling around in the air, the jet trooper screamed as he smashed into a rock and his jet pack exploded.

No cheers came from BB-8 this time, only cries of distress. There was a reason for the soft landing—everyone was sinking into black sand. Poe cursed, unable to wiggle out.

Rey found her own legs being sucked down into a pit. "Sinking fields, like on Jakku! Grab on to something!"

Chewbacca whined as struggling only made it worse. C-3PO was down to his waist. "What an ignoble end!"

Beeping the whole while, BB-8 spun until the black sand enveloped him. Poe went under next. Finn tried to keep his head above the surface. "Rey, I never told you, I—"

"What?"

The sand muted his response. C-3PO didn't even get a final complaint as his vocabulator was clogged.

Chewbacca reached out to Rey. Human and Wookiee hands touched, and then sand poured over her and she was reminded of home, one last time.

CHAPTER 9

THE SAND GOT in Rey's nose, her eyes, her ears, and her mouth. Black, gritty stuff that choked her breath, abraded her skin. She began to panic, and the more she struggled with her legs and arms, the more she was sucked down into the pit.

But then she could move her foot, and her leg, and then both feet and both legs, until the lower half of her body was free and she was sliding down through a chute of sand—*whoosh*. She felt air instead of sand and then—*thwack*—she landed on solid ground so hard her spine rattled.

"You all right?" Poe stood over her in a dark cavern, dimly lit from the holes in the quicksand above. He offered Rey his hand.

She took it and rose to her feet, brushing off sand. "Where's Finn?"

"Where's Chewie?" Poe asked.

"You didn't say my name, sir, but I'm all right," C-3PO said, standing up. Sand crusted his plating.

Behind them, a long shaggy form fell through the ceiling to thud onto the ground. The pained groan was all Wookiee.

But he managed to stand and shake off the sand. BB-8 rolled nearby and whistled.

Finn emerged from a tunnel. "What is this place?"

"This isn't the afterlife, is it?" C-3PO asked. "Are droids allowed here?"

Poe glanced at the ceiling. Sand drizzled down, but the holes were closing. "I thought we were goners."

"We might still be, sir," C-3PO said.

Finn looked around the cavern. "So which way is out?"

Rey extended her lightsaber. The blue blade provided some illumination. Poe switched on his glowrod, which gave them a little more.

The currents of the Force swirled in the cavern, in ways Rey didn't understand. They tugged her toward the tunnel, and she didn't question it. "This way."

Rey held up her lightsaber and took the lead. The tunnel was circular in structure with segmented ridges, as if something had burrowed through the ground. She remembered a story a trader on Jakku had once told her about a sand serpent called the vexis. It dwelled in Pasaana's desert and was generally peaceful unless provoked, but if it was, "You can count your mortal breaths," the trader had said. Rey didn't recall anything about it living underground, however.

"I don't want to know what made these tunnels," Poe muttered.

C-3PO canted his head to look upward. "Judging by the bore circumference, any number of deadly species could—"

Poe cut him off. "I said did not want to know. *Not.*"

On Minfar, they had encountered the grobel, a grub-like creature that had dug similar tunnels through the planet's underground—and gobbled up anything living before it.

As they went around a turn, Rey walked close to Finn. "So what was it? What were you going to tell me?"

Finn studied the tunnel. "When?"

She sensed he was trying to dodge her question. "When you were sinking in the sand, you said, 'I never told you.'"

Finn wouldn't look her in the eye. "I'll tell you later."

But Poe had been listening. "When you're not around me?"

"Yeah," Finn said.

Poe shook his head. "Great. We're going to die in sand burrows and we're all keeping secrets."

"I'll tell you when you tell us about all that shifty stuff you know how to do," Finn said.

A sharp beep from BB-8 stopped the argument and drew everyone's attention toward a smashed-up vehicle in the tunnel ahead of them. "Is that a speeder?" Finn asked.

Rey stepped forward to shine her blade on the wreckage. "An old one," she said. It gave her a strange feeling.

"Perhaps we'll find the driver," C-3PO said.

BB-8 trilled something snarky. "Yep, BB-8, I think dead, too," Poe said. Chewbacca barked in agreement.

None of their sarcasm dulled C-3PO's curiosity. He toddled up to the speeder and examined an ornament decorating its hood. "Oh my! A hex charm!"

Poe wrinkled his brow. "A what?"

C-3PO backed away from the speeder, no longer curious. "A common emblem of Sith loyalists."

"Sith . . ." Rey repeated in a low voice. Was that what had pulled her into this tunnel? The dark side?

"This was Ochi's?" Finn asked, indicating the speeder.

Rey searched her feelings. Oddly, even with the hex charm, the dark side seemed faded and distant, like background noise in the Force. But the noise gave her insight. "Luke sensed it," she said. "Ochi never left this place."

"And he ended up down here," Finn said.

Poe looked back the way they had come. "He was headed from his ship. Same thing happened to us, happened to him."

"Sinking fields," Finn said, repeating Rey's words on the surface. "So how did Ochi get out?"

Rey looked past the wreckage and realized what she felt in the tunnel wasn't the dark side—it was death. "He didn't."

On the tunnel floor lay a humanoid skull, a skeleton, and the shells of gouge beetles that had devoured the flesh.

C-3PO bent forward to take a closer took. "Bones. Never a good sign."

"Bones, I don't like bones," Poe said, looking away.

A beep from BB-8 drew Rey over to a pile of what had to be Ochi's belongings. She sifted through shredded clothes and pulled out a leather belt. A knife sheath hung on the belt. From it Rey pulled a wicked-looking dagger with an arrowhead-shaped blade. Her hand became cold, deathly cold, as she held it, and she heard the distant echo of screams. "Horrible things have happened with this," she said. "Horrible things."

Poe aimed his glowrod at the dagger. Runes had been chiseled into the blade. "There's writing on it," he said.

"Perhaps I can translate," C-3PO offered.

Rey couldn't bear holding the dagger any longer, so she gave it to C-3PO. He held the blade to the light, clearly more comfortable with it than she was, and examined the runes.

"Lovely metalwork . . . oh! The location of the wayfinder has been inscribed upon this dagger—it's the clue that Master Luke was looking for!"

"And where's the wayfinder?" Poe asked.

"I'm afraid I cannot tell you," C-3PO said.

Poe got heated. "Twenty point three fa-zillion languages and you can't read that?"

"Oh, I have read it, sir. I know exactly where the way-finder is," C-3PO said, his enthusiasm undiminished. "Unfortunately, it's written in the runic language of the Sith."

"So what?" Rey said, starting to get heated herself.

The droid's joints creaked when he turned to her. "My programming forbids me from translating it."

Poe looked like he was about to disassemble the droid. "You're telling us the one time we need you to talk, you can't?"

"I am mechanically incapable of speaking translations

from the Sith. My vocal processors cannot phonate the words." A shadow, large and sinuous in shape, with eyes that glittered like fire-gems, grew in the tunnel behind C-3PO as he droned on. " I believe the rule was passed by the Senate of the Old Republic—"

BB-8 scooted behind Rey. Chewbacca raised his bowcaster. Noticing something was amiss, C-3PO finally turned—and cried out so loud that static crackled through his vocoder. "Serpent, serpent, serpent!" He dropped the dagger and shuffled back over to the group.

The creature opened a jaw full of giant fangs and hissed. Looking at the beast, Rey knew the trader's story was not a tall tale. The vexis was real.

Poe drew his blaster, but Rey pushed it down so he wouldn't fire. She stared into the creature's eyes and held her saber out before her, but did not attack.

"Don't you want to use that thing?" Poe asked.

Rey didn't respond. The vexis lifted its head high over them and hissed again, lashing them with a wind that blew Chewbacca's fur and pushed BB-8 backward.

Rey locked her gaze on the vexis's eyes. Something in them told her that things were not what they seemed.

She handed Finn her lightsaber. Taking a step forward, she relied on what she'd forgotten when sinking into the quicksand—her training.

"Rey—" Finn said.

She tuned him out and walked toward the vexis. Its

head hovered above her, yet it did not strike. Reflected in its jewel-like eyes, Rey saw something other than aggression. She saw pain. "It might be injured."

"And it might just be a giant killer sand snake," Poe groused.

"More light," Rey ordered.

Poe aimed the glowrod in her direction. Light shone over the scaled body of the vexis, revealing an oozing, bloody wound. The pain Rey had seen in those eyes was real.

She came close enough to touch the vexis. "Leia says when something's trying to hurt you, it was usually hurt by something bigger," she said to everyone, including herself.

The vexis hissed a third time—at her—its fangs gleaming. Rey wavered, but she did not break focus from those eyes. Through the Force, she calmed herself but also tried to do the same for the beast. She let it know that she meant it no harm, that she would help it.

When the vexis did not bite, Rey reached out and put her hand on the wound.

Relying on instinct more than any technique she'd read in the Jedi texts, she closed her eyes and conferred her own warmth into the vexis's wound. She imagined giving its cells energy to accelerate the healing process. Feeling the wound start to stitch, she committed more of herself to the beast, taking some of its pain and exhaling it through her mouth. When she opened her eyes, the wound no longer bled.

The vexis lowered its head to her face. She did not back

away as it opened its mouth. The forked tongue came out and the vexis hissed, tousling her hair.

The serpent then squeezed itself around the tunnel and slithered away.

Finn and Poe were staring at her in amazement, but Rey was more concerned with her hand. She wiggled her fingers and winced. Her whole hand ached from the healing.

BB-8 whirled around her and beeped a question. "I just transferred a bit of life, Force energy from me to him," she explained. "You would've done the same."

Finn pointed farther down the tunnel, where the vexis had burrowed a hole in the ceiling to the surface. "Well, we've got our way out."

Chewbacca picked up the dagger and slipped it into his satchel. Then they all followed the vexis's trail through the tunnel and out the hole. Reaching the surface, they saw no sign of the sand serpent.

Ochi's spaceship was parked at the top of a rocky butte. They climbed up the slope, with Chewbacca carrying BB-8 under his arm. C-3PO brought up the rear.

"Hurry it up!" Poe urged. "We've got to find someone who can translate that dagger, like a helpful droid."

C-3PO didn't seem to process the put-down. He had stopped to stare at the rusty transport at the top of the ridge. "We cannot possibly fly in that old wreck. I suggest we return to the *Millennium Falcon* at once."

"They'll be waiting for us at the *Falcon*," Poe said.

Finn nodded in assent. "If they catch us, they'll send us to the pits of Griq."

"Yeah, and use you as a target droid," Poe said to C-3PO.

"You both make excellent points, at times," C-3PO said. He started ascending the ridge again, moving faster than Rey thought possible.

While the others went with the droid, Rey paused. Something dark and sinister rippled through the Force, coming not from the ship but somewhere else.

"I'll be right behind you," she said to the others.

Finn stopped a few steps away and looked at her. Rey handed him her satchel. "I'll be okay." She could tell he wasn't reassured. But she couldn't waste time explaining.

Rey turned and walked into the center of the plateau. She stood there, waiting, breathing. Her breaths were short and quick, her heartbeat rapid in her chest. On the horizon, a black speck grew to a dot.

She employed the calming techniques Luke had taught her. Deep inhalations and long exhalations, in and out, in and out. They slowed down her breathing and her heart so she was in control of both.

That dot on the horizon was now a ball with sharp-edged wings. And it was approaching all too fast.

Rey knew what it was. She knew who was in it. The Force told her these things before her eyes or ears could.

Kylo Ren's TIE fighter sped across the desert toward her.

Rey unclipped her lightsaber, squared her shoulders, and stood to meet it. He must have sensed her because the

TIE accelerated. It raced less than a meter over the desert surface, swirling up a cyclone of sand behind it.

Igniting her lightsaber, Rey turned away from the TIE.

She crouched into a fighting stance. The TIE screamed at her from behind. The engines of Ochi's freighter roared to life nearby. All those sounds faded away as she concentrated on her breath. The Force flowed through her, starting as a tingle and becoming a torrent, surging from her heart to her limbs.

She glanced back, once, daring the TIE to come at her, and then did the unthinkable. She sprinted away from it.

Rey ran with all her muscle and her might. Her lightsaber flashed before her and her boots kicked up sand and dust. For a moment, she was back on Jakku, fleeing scavenger gangs who wanted to rob her of finds. She might have escaped them, but she'd never outrace a TIE fighter. Not even her talents in the Force could match twin ion engines.

The Force, however, could help her do other things.

When the TIE was nearly upon her, the sharp points of its wings mere meters away from staking her body, Rey gritted her teeth, raised her hands above her head, and leapt.

Not forward but backward. The Force gave her lift.

Somersaulting in midair, she flung herself over the TIE while slashing down with her lightsaber blade. She landed on her feet, facing the rear of the cockpit.

Ren's TIE sped onward—and then one of the wing rods crumpled, due to an expert slice from Rey's saber. The wing smashed the ground and broke off, the TIE careened, and then the same thing happened to its other wing. But the TIE cockpit kept going, tearing through the desert sands, a wingless ball rolling over itself.

Rey deactivated her blade and watched the dust cloud disappear. She could only hope that was the end of Kylo Ren, but she doubted it.

Finn ran toward her. "Rey! They got Chewie!"

She blinked. Finn pointed at the sky, where a First Order troop transport flew toward the clouds. "He's in there!"

A hurled lightsaber or a blaster shot wouldn't stop an armored transport, and Rey was too far from Ochi's craft to pursue them in time. This left her with only one option.

Rey extended her hand toward the transport. If the Force could move mountains, it could move starships.

She called on the Force to apply it at its most fundamental level—as a force. Channeling it through her, she tried to wrench the transport back to the planet.

The transport stalled in the air. Its engines sputtered. It was attempting to move forward, but she held it back. Her body trembled, her mind and muscles ached from the strain, but she could bring the transport down, she knew she could. And slowly the transport started to descend, meter by meter, toward the ground.

Then another force yanked it in the other direction.

The transport's engines blazed. Rey nearly lost her grip. She tightened her hold on it and pulled, taxing her body to the limit. She recognized her opponent from the crude way the Force was being used.

Kylo Ren.

He stood as a silhouette in the distance, near the smoking wreck of his TIE cockpit, seemingly unhurt.

He pulled and she pulled, like two opposing tractor beams, with the transport caught in the middle. Its engines whined, threatening to burst. Something would have to give soon. She had little strength left.

But she couldn't let the First Order take Chewbacca. Before they killed him, they'd make him suffer in every conceivable way. She couldn't allow another hero from the stories of her youth, another friend, to perish because of Kylo Ren.

She pulled with every last fiber of her being. The strain was enormous. Blood rushed to her head. Her face drew taut and red. Her neck swelled. Storms roared in her ears. But even with all her exertion, Kylo Ren proved stronger. The transport was beginning to pull away from her.

That brute. He had ordered the slaughter of peaceful villagers on Jakku. He had tortured Poe, tortured her, forced himself into her memories. He had murdered his own father. And now he was about to wreak his vengeance upon Chewbacca.

Her anger at him for what he had done—and what he would do—reached a breaking point. From it erupted a power she didn't realize she had. She almost screamed as it coursed from her hands, a shock of blue electricity that lanced upward and struck the transport like a lightning bolt.

A lightning bolt might have fizzled against the ship's shields, but this was no ordinary lightning bolt. It was the raw energy of the Force, directed by her anger. It went right through the shields into the reactor core.

Voices cried out in the Force as the transport exploded.

Rey staggered back from the fireball in the sky. Pieces of the ship crashed around her like meteors. She stood there in disbelief, not fully comprehending what had just happened.

Then it hit her. "Chewie!" she screamed.

He was in that ship and she had killed him. Inadvertently, perhaps, but she had done it all the same. Her anger at Kylo Ren had veered into hatred and had overwhelmed her other impulses.

"Rey!" Poe called out. "We have to go!"

She turned from the horror she'd caused. Poe stood on the ramp of Ochi's ship and motioned to the sky. First Order TIEs and transports dove at them in rapid fashion.

Rey struggled with the words. "But Chewie—he—I—"

"Now!" he yelled.

The First Order ships were almost upon them. She ran to Ochi's ship, Finn with her.

The main hold of the vessel was dark and dingy. Sand covered the floor. Rey found a corner and sat in it, letting Poe, Finn, and BB-8 handle the piloting duties.

The cabin shook as the ship lifted. Rey hardly noticed. Her thoughts were elsewhere.

No wonder Luke had not wanted to teach her. No wonder Leia had wanted her to stay and to keep training. They saw the darkness within her—and she had failed them.

/// CHAPTER 10

CHEWBACCA WAS DEAD.

Finn couldn't believe it. It had happened so fast, with so little warning, that it didn't seem real.

After Rey had said she was right behind them, Finn had boarded Ochi's freighter with Poe, Chewbacca, and the droids. In a rare stroke of luck, the ship's fuel cells had not dried up despite years of exposure to the desert heat. Poe was able to activate the systems and fire up the engines. But Rey still hadn't come aboard, so Chewbacca headed out to get her. When he didn't come back, Finn went looking for both of them. He had a hunch Kylo Ren was involved—only someone with his power could stop a full-grown Wookiee and a girl as gifted in the Force as Rey.

Coming around a ridge, Finn spotted not Ren but two mercenaries in mismatched armor. They had Chewbacca in shackles and hauled him before a First Order transport surrounded by stormtroopers. Finn nearly rushed them until he recognized he didn't stand a chance. He'd be eating sand before he made it halfway to them. So he did the next best thing—he went looking for Rey.

He found her on the other side of Ochi's ship, staring at a dust cloud of a demolished TIE far in the desert. By then it seemed almost too late, since the First Order transport was rising into the sky. But Rey found a way to stop the transport. In a display of power that astounded Finn, she used the Force to pull the ship backward. She would have brought it to the ground, if not for Kylo Ren. He had emerged from the TIE wreckage to pit his power against hers.

That was when the strain had seemed too much for Rey. Blue energy erupted from her hands, enveloping the transport and causing it to crash.

She had boarded Ochi's freighter after Finn, but then slouched in the corner and didn't move, even after they escaped Pasaana. Finn tried talking to her, but she wouldn't listen to him. He went to help Poe in the cockpit, pushing whatever buttons and flicking whatever switches Poe asked him to push and flick. The pilot had mastered the controls very quickly. They'd even learned the ship's name—*Bestoon Legacy*—from the onboard computer. What that legacy was, given Ochi's past, Finn didn't care to know.

While Poe ran tests, Finn checked on Rey in the main hold. She was standing up, looking at the palm of her hand under the compartment lights. Beside her BB-8 moaned while C-3PO repeated, "Poor, poor Chewbacca."

Finn remembered the time he had tended Chewbacca's injuries in the *Millennium Falcon*'s medbay. Gangsters had shot the Wookiee in the shoulder, yet he thrashed and howled under Finn's care as if all the fur on his shaggy body had been blaster-burned. But Finn had survived that test of Wookiee rage to proudly become one of Chewbacca's closest friends. And Finn knew the big lug would be roaring in his grave if he learned Rey blamed herself for his death.

"It wasn't your fault," Finn insisted.

Her gaze remained on her hand. "It was."

"No," Finn said. "It was Ren. He made you—"

"Chewie's gone." Rey spun around to face him. "That power came from me. I lost control."

Finn shook his head. What she was saying was nonsense. If Kylo Ren hadn't attacked, Chewbacca would be alive.

"Finn, there are things you don't know," she said.

"Then tell me."

"I had a vision when I was training. Of the throne of the Sith," she said. "I saw who was on it."

"Ren?"

"And me," she said.

BB-8 let out an inquisitive beep while investigating a pile of Ochi's old clothes. He extended the gripper from his tool-arm and pulled back a tattered black cloth. Under it lay a small droid with a conical head and a treaded, wheel-shaped body. Rust speckled its parts and it had dents everywhere, like it had been dropped or kicked.

With a triumphant beep, BB-8 jump-started the smaller droid's power cell. "Battery charged!" it said in a sped-up voice. It spun on its tread, rolling over to Rey. "Hello, hello!"

"Hello." She reached down to touch it.

It zipped away. "No thank you."

Rey glanced at BB-8 and Finn. "Looks like someone treated him badly." She turned back to the conical droid. "It's all right. You're with us now. We won't hurt you."

Poe came out of the cockpit, adjusting his pilots' gloves. "We're running out of time. What are we going to do?"

"We've got to go back to base," Finn said.

"We don't have time to go back," Poe said. "We're not giving up. If we do, Chewie died for nothing."

"Poe, Chewie had the dagger—"

"Then we've got to find another way," Poe said.

"There isn't," Finn said. "That was the only clue to the wayfinder and it's gone."

"So true," C-3PO said wistfully. "The inscription lives only in my memory now."

Poe and Finn looked at each other. Rey kept quiet, sitting on a crate. "Hold on," Poe said. "The inscription that was on the dagger is in your memory?"

"Yes, Master Poe. But a translation from a forbidden language cannot be retrieved. That is, short of a complete redactive memory bypass."

"A complete *what*?" Finn detested techno jargon.

"It's a terribly dangerous and sinful act performed on unwitting droid by dregs and criminals."

"Let's do that," Finn said.

Poe mulled it over. "I know a black-market droidsmith."

C-3PO's wistful tone turned worried. "Black-market droidsmith?"

Poe ignored the droid. "But he's on Kijimi."

"What's wrong with Kijimi?" Finn asked.

"I've had bad luck on Kijimi." Poe frowned, then took a breath. "But . . . if this mission fails, it's all been for nothing, all we've done, all this time."

What Finn was about to say, he wouldn't have said a few months before. Having a family, even a motley one like the Resistance, had changed things. "We're *all* in this," he said, turning to Rey, "to the end."

Rey looked at him, then slid off the crate and stood.

"For Chewie," Rey said.

Finn offered a hand to Poe and a hand to Rey. Both accepted. "For Chewie," Poe said.

C-3PO clinked over to them and held out his metal hands. Rey took one; Finn took the other. The droid's grip was firm and surprisingly warm. "For the Wookiee," he said.

In that moment, Finn felt a glow around him. It was as if his faith in his friends and their faith in him gave him a newfound strength. He'd trained for years with fellow storm-troopers of his batch, had blood brothers like Slip and Nines, yet never once had he shared a bond like this.

Was this what Rey meant when she talked about feeling the Force?

CHAPTER 11

POE'S BAD LUCK on Kijimi might be changing. He had found a route to the droidsmith's workshop that stayed clear of the First Order's checkpoints. The biggest challenge to the group would be skirting past the storm-troopers who patrolled the city.

He pulled the hood of his jacket tighter around his head as he hurried down the lantern-lit street. It was cold in the mountain capital, colder than he remembered. It was also quieter. Much quieter. He had just passed Monk's Gate, and it seemed as if the silence of the monks who had built the place centuries before had returned. The Kijimi City Poe knew had abounded with a rowdy and rambunctious crowd even on snowy nights, but that boisterous spirit seemed to be broken. The few Poe passed largely kept to themselves. Occasionally a face would peer out from a window of one of the stone buildings, then quickly disappear. The city that had once celebrated its lawlessness had been subjected to the most ruthless of laws.

Martial law.

The First Order had installed a garrison there to

suppress rebel activity and prey on the population. Three-legged walkers and their snowtrooper complements were out in full force, harassing locals and raiding homes. One patrol ripped a daughter from her mother, no doubt to be taken to training facilities and brainscraped into one of the First Order's loyal soldiers. This was what must have happened to Finn, years before, though he didn't talk about it.

Poe couldn't imagine being taken from his parents. His boyhood on Yavin 4, before his mother died, had been a happy one. His mother had taught him how to fly her A-wing when he was barely six years old, and from his father he'd learned the art of stealth, which kept him alive in situations like this.

As the troopers carried away the crying girl, Poe wished he could do something. But if he revealed himself, he'd put the Resistance in danger. If they were going to defeat this evil, they had to do more than outwit a stormtrooper patrol; they had to bring about the downfall of the First Order.

Poe slipped past another patrol and turned into an alcove where his friends waited. They all wore the long coats Poe had stolen from a guildhouse. Rey and Finn shivered and exhaled clouds from under their hoods; C-3PO's photoreceptors shone under his. BB-8 and Ochi's small cone-faced droid stayed mostly out of sight at their feet.

"They're everywhere," Poe said, glancing at the troopers who marched past. "We gotta find another way around."

"We should leave," C-3PO suggested. Since arriving on Kijimi, the droid had reverted to his usual anxious state.

"Clam it, Threepio," Poe said, and gestured to everyone. "Follow me."

Poe led the group through the city, keeping to the back streets to avoid patrols. After a long and winding path, they came to an alley. "All right," he said. "Let's head down this—"

A blaster muzzle sprang from the shadows and pressed into Poe's neck. "Heard you were spotted at Monk's Gate," the aggressor said, her voice filtered through a helmet processor. "I thought, 'He's not stupid enough to come back here.'"

Poe recognized the blaster's bronzium barrel just as he recognized the bronzium helmet and temperature-regulating body glove worn by his former partner. "Oh, you'd be surprised," he said, half serious.

Finn stepped back with BB-8 and Ochi's droid. "What's going on?"

Rey gripped the staff she had partially concealed under her coat, eyeing Poe's assailant. "Who's this?"

"Guys, this is Zorii," Poe said. "Zorii, this is Rey, Finn—"

Zorii didn't let him finish. "I could pull the trigger right now."

"I've seen you do worse," Poe said.

"For a lot less." Zorrii's finger quivered on the trigger.

Sarcasm clearly wasn't going to solve this. Poe pushed down his hood and slowly turned toward her. "Can we just talk about this?"

"I want to see your brains in the snow," she said.

The polarized viewplate of Zorii's helmet obscured her face, but Poe could tell she was ticked off enough that she might forget about their good times together and actually pull the trigger. "Zorii, we could use your help," he pleaded. "We gotta crack this droid's head open and fast."

C-3PO, still under his hood, swiveled to stare at Poe. "Pardon me!"

Poe didn't pay the droid any attention. "We're trying to find Babu Frik," he explained.

"Babu," Zorii said. "Babu only works for the crew. That's not you anymore."

"What crew?" Rey demanded.

The bandit looked at Rey. "Funny he never mentioned it. Your friend's old job was running spice."

Finn stared at Poe in disbelief. "You were a *spice runner*?"

"You were a stormtrooper?" Poe countered, falling back on sarcasm.

Rey did not appear amused. "*Were* you a spice runner?"

"Were you a scavenger?" Poe quipped. "We could do this all night."

"You don't have all night. You don't even have now." Zorii walked around him, keeping the blaster aimed at his head. "I'm still digging out of the hole you put me in when you left to join the cause."

Moving closer to Rey, Zorii took a hard look at the girl's face under the hood. "You. You're the girl they're looking for. Bounty for you might just cover us."

Two menacing thugs approached, carrying equally menacing pikes. "*Djak'kankah*," Zorii commanded.

"No *djak'kankah*," Poe said, for all the good it would do.

Before Zorri could pull the trigger, Rey whipped out her quarterstaff and knocked the pistol out of Zorii's hand. She then swung the staff around to thump an onrushing thug flat in the face. The thug fell back, and Rey pivoted, tossing her staff at the second thug. That goon also collapsed, whacked in the head.

Rey then drew her lightsaber and pointed the humming blue blade at Zorii's throat. "We really could use your help," she said. "Please." Her manners masked her threat.

The girl from Jakku never failed to impress Poe. She might be a scavenger, but she was indeed the best fighter the Resistance had. And if he was impressed, he knew Zorii would be, too. After a long look at Rey, the bandit professed as much. "Not that you care, but I like you," Zorii said.

Rey stared down the length of her blade at Zorii. "I care," she said, then deactivated her saber.

Zorii picked up her blaster and holstered it. "We can get to Babu's through the Thieves' Quarter." She headed down the alley, and Poe and the others went after her.

Finn walked beside Poe, shaking his head. "Poe Dameron, spice runner."

"Don't," Poe whispered.

Finn smirked and kept needling. "Runner of spice . . ."

"*All right*," Poe said, rather loudly. He was never going to live this one down.

Yet he was still alive. Zorii had almost pulled the trigger. But she hadn't.

Maybe his luck on Kijimi was changing.

Kylo Ren exited the interrogation cell on the *Steadfast*, leaving Chewbacca slumped on the floor, moaning in pain. General Hux, Admiral Griss, and Allegiant General Pryde were waiting for Ren in the hall.

They followed Ren as he walked down the corridor. "I want all the Wookiee's belongings brought to my quarters," he said.

Pryde nodded, seeming particularly pleased with himself. "Sir, the Knights of Ren have tracked the scavenger."

"To a settlement called Kijimi," Griss added.

"They're searching there now," Pryde said.

Eager as ever, Hux tried to take the advantage. "Shall we destroy the city, Supreme—"

Ren lifted one finger at the general, quieting him. "Set a course for Kijimi. I want her taken alive."

He strode out of the detention area. No one followed him this time.

CHAPTER 12

C-3PO WAS EMBARRASSED.

Some might say that would be an impossibility, because droids were not programmed for shame. But C-3PO possessed a protocol module that had evolved from decades of interaction with fellow beings. If he could assess anything, it would be an embarrassing circumstance. And sitting on an examination table with the back of his headplate removed and his parts showing was the definition of embarrassing.

"If you'll pardon me for saying so," he said to Mistress Rey, "I haven't the faintest idea why I agreed to this. I must be malfunctioning."

The young woman touched his shoulder and regarded him with a human expression of sympathy. "You're going to be okay," she said. His auditory sensors detected apprehension in her voice, increasing the odds that he might not emerge from Babu Frik's experiments intact.

The long-whiskered droidsmith, barely as big as C-3PO's head, hopped around an examination table, muttering in his own language while jamming wires into C-3PO's exposed cranium. Bursts of electrical current generated a hum in

C-3PO's verbobrain that made comprehensive analysis difficult. Much preferable to all this would be a dip in the lubricant pool that bubbled in the corner.

The bath was the only thing that looked inviting in Babu's workshop, which was located in the back room of a seedy cantina. Random droid parts and equipment cluttered much of the space, filling shelves or hanging off ceiling hooks. Mistress Rey and the others had to be careful not to trip over a wayward mouse droid or lean against a workbench that wasn't just a workbench but an actual K1-RF maintenance unit. Most distressing for C-3PO was the deactivated B1 battle droid gathering rust near the door while the dome of an R5 astromech unit supported a scrap pile.

Is this how C-3PO would end up, deactivated and discarded in a junk heap like Jawa salvage? His estimator couldn't tell him the odds—Babu Frik's electroprobe had overloaded it.

On low power, C-3PO devoted what independent processing he had left to listen to his human counterparts. "Zorii, is this really going to work? Can Babu help us?" Rey asked the acquaintance of Master Dameron, who disregarded custom and wore her helmet inside.

Zorii spoke to Babu in his guttural tongue. The droidsmith answered as he soldered sockets on C-3PO's head, but C-3PO couldn't understand since his expanded language database had been disconnected. Fortunately, Zorii interpreted the answer.

"Babu says he's found something in your droid's

forbidden memory bank. Words translated from"—Zorii hesitated—"*Sith*?"

"Yes," Rey said.

Master Finn nodded. "That's what we need."

Zorii turned to look at Master Dameron, who was descending a flight of stairs. "Who are you hanging out with that speaks Sith?" C-3PO registered a degree of shock in her filtered voice.

"Can he make him translate it?" Master Dameron asked. "Babu, can you make him translate it?"

Zorii posed the question to Babu in his language, who replied as he tinkered with C-3PO's neural contacts. "Yes," Zorii said, "but doing so will trigger a—"

Her comment initiated C-3PO's self-preservation routine. He rotated his head toward the humans and finished Zorii's sentence with her. "Complete memory wipe."

Master Dameron stared at C-3PO, though it was hard to read the human's expression. "You're saying we make him translate and he won't remember anything?"

"Droid remember go blank," the droidsmith said in his pidgin Basic. "Blankblank. Zero."

C-3PO's self-preservation routine again provoked him to speak up. "Oh, there must be some other way." The last time he'd had a wipe, he had lost all memory of his maker.

"Doesn't Artoo back up your memory?" Finn asked.

The mere consideration of what that implied threatened to short-circuit C-3PO's central processor. "Please, sir," he said. "Artoo's storage units are famously unreliable."

Mistress Rey looked at the droid. Her expression remained sympathetic. "You know the odds better than any of us. Do we have a choice?"

For a million microseconds, C-3PO heard nothing from anyone. Even Babu Frik ceased his muttering. When one of them did speak, the response came from a most unlikely source.

Himself.

"If this mission fails," C-3PO said, standing up, his power reserves straining to access memory of a recent event, "it was all for naught. All we've done. All this time."

The droid angled his head toward Mistress Rey, Master Finn, and then Master Dameron, whose expression was not difficult to read at this moment. The pilot seemed genuinely surprised. "Threepio, what are you doing?" he asked.

C-3PO brightened his photoreceptors. "Taking one last look, sir, at my friends."

Seeing them before him, concerned for his safety, C-3PO received a surge of power that overrode his self-preservation routine and briefly reconnected his linguistic database.

"*Ti'takka ollana*," he said to Babu Frik in his native Anzellan, and laid down on the table. "You may proceed."

As Babu began the procedure, C-3PO's secondary processor, which had been running in the background, computed a workaround that would bypass the security routines for translation. "I just had an idea," C-3PO said. "There's something else we could try—"

There was a spark and the optical registers of his photo-receptors went dark.

While Babu Frik operated on C-3PO, Rey sat away from the action and snacked on berries she had plucked en route to the workshop. BB-8 nestled next to her, but the droid from Ochi's ship, who was designated D-O, couldn't stop moving. The sparks and sounds of Babu Frik's thermtorch agitated the small droid so much that he spun back and forth on his monowheel, his parts grating against each other from years of disuse. "Squeaky wheel," he repeated over and over. "I have a squeaky wheel."

Rey rose and took a lubricant bottle from a shelf. When she crouched down to D-O's level, the droid shuddered. "It's just oil," she said. "Won't hurt. I promise."

She sprayed around his joints and in between his cooling vents. D-O didn't have many complex parts. His design was simple, the kind sold in hobbyist kits. She would've loved to have built one as a kid.

D-O started moving again, without the grinding noises. "Squeak eliminated!" he said. "Thank you very much! Very kind!" He made an appreciative squeal and ran rings around BB-8. It made Rey happy.

Then she remembered what her help had done to Chewbacca.

Finn walked over and nudged her. He knew what she was thinking. She was terrible at hiding it.

She forced a smile again and watched D-O enjoy his freedom. He had been locked on that dusty transport for so long, he'd probably thought that he'd never roll around again. She understood. After her parents had left her, she had spent many long nights pondering if there was anything more for her, too.

Reminded of that horrible memory of abandonment, she had a sudden realization. "I know where I've seen it, the ship he was on," she said to Finn as D-O wheeled about them. "Ochi's ship. The day my parents left, they were on that ship."

Finn seemed as shocked as she was. "Are you sure?"

She never got to answer him. Zorii and Poe ran down the stairs from where they'd been keeping lookout on the rooftop. "There's an incoming Destroyer," Zorii said.

"We gotta move now," Poe said. "Babu, did you get it?"

Huge sparks from Babu's thermtorch startled the group. C-3PO's photoreceptors flickered and glowed a sinister red.

"Yes, droid is ready," Babu Frik said. "Droid unlock!"

C-3PO sat up on the examination table and spoke in a voice that didn't sound at all like his, but was deeper and darker in tone. "The Emperor's wayfinder is sealed inside the Imperial vaults. At delta-three-six transient nine-three-six, bearing three-two on a moon in the system of Endor. From the southern shore, only this blade tells. Only this blade tells—" His voice clicked and his photoreceptors switched off, yet he continued to sit on the table, frozen mid-sentence.

Finn dispelled the momentary confusion. "The Endor system? Where the last war ended?"

Babu hopped from one splayed foot to the other. "Endor! I know this. Babu will help!"

The components in the workshop started to shake. Rey rushed up the stairs to the rooftop. A massive First Order warship blocked out most of the night sky above Kijimi City.

The rumbling and rattling increased. Droid pieces tumbled off shelves and fell from their ceiling hooks.

Rey stared up at the Star Destroyer. Ren was aboard—and she could feel his anger. "Ren's Destroyer," she said.

"He's here?" Finn asked from the bottom of the stairs.

Not just Ren. Rey also felt the mind of someone dear to her, a mind that had been attacked by Kylo Ren. The pain of that invasion rippled through the Force. "Chewie."

"What about him?" Finn asked.

"He's on Ren's ship. He's alive."

"What? How?"

"He's alive!" She turned to look back down the stairs. "Finn, he must've been on a different transport."

"Then we gotta go get him!" Finn said.

Zorii stood near Finn at the staircase. She glanced at Poe. "Your friend's on that Destroyer, sky trash?"

"I guess he is," Poe said, letting slip a rare smile.

A loud, electrical zap sounded from C-3PO. There was another click, and his photoreceptors illuminated to their normal yellow brightness. "Allow me to introduce myself," he said, his well-mannered accent having returned. "I am

See-Threepio, human-cyborg relations. And you are?"

Everyone glanced at each other and no one reintroduced themselves. "Okay," Poe said, "that's gonna be a problem."

"Hello, I Babu Frik," the droidsmith said to his patient.

C-3PO turned to him. "Why, hello!"

More parts fell from the shelves. Cracks appeared in the wall. The Destroyer's repulsors could churn up the workshop without the ship ever dropping a bomb.

"The alleys," Zorii said. "Let's go."

As Finn and Poe helped C-3PO, Rey glanced back at the Destroyer through the window. Chewbacca was alive. And she was going to rescue him.

Poe raced after Zorii through a maze of alleys outside Babu Frik's workshop. First Order troopers seemed to be everywhere, yet Poe's former spice-running partner knew where to go to avoid them. Rey, Finn, BB-8, and even Ochi's droid kept up. C-3PO, as usual, lagged behind.

"Threepio, move your bronze butt!" Poe yelled.

C-3PO waddled down the alley on his stiff legs. "How dare you! We've only just met!"

Zorii halted at the mouth of the alley. She looked around the corner and then nodded to Rey that the area was clear. Rey, Finn, and the droids hurried out of the alley, with C-3PO taking the rear.

Poe was about to go after them, but Zorii held him back. She handed him perhaps the most valuable thing she possessed, a First Order captain's medallion. "Might get you on a capital ship," she said. "Might help your friend."

The medallion was a circular device embedded with circuitry. It transmitted a subspace code that gave a ship free passage through a blockade or landing rights at a First Order facility. Zorii had shown it to Poe when they were on lookout on Babu's roof. She'd said she was going to use it to take the blocked hyperlanes and find a home not occupied by the First Order.

Poe knew it was her only ticket off-world to start a new life. "I don't think I can take this from you."

"I don't care what you think," she said.

Rey called back to them. "Poe—come on!"

Poe noticed some armored figures rapidly approaching them from a cross street. They didn't look like stormtroopers, but the First Order was known to employ other enforcers.

He pocketed the medallion and looked at Zorii. Hours earlier, she had nearly killed him. Now she was sacrificing her future, and probably her life, to rescue him.

"Can I kiss you?" he asked, and not in jest.

"Go," she said.

He didn't want to, but he did, running after Rey and the others. He owed so much to Zorii. When he had left Yavin 4 after his mother's death, Zorii had taken him under her wing and taught him all the tricks of the trade his parents hadn't. Sure, they had broken a few laws together and run spice with some crooks, but she had helped make him the man he was.

He looked back. Zorii had dashed off.

He'd probably never see her green eyes again.

Chewbacca was alive.

It didn't seem possible. Finn had seen Chewie escorted toward the transport. He had seen that same transport explode. Granted, he hadn't seen the Wookiee physically board the transport, but there was hardly enough time in between him running to find Rey and actually finding her for Chewbacca to be transferred.

Had he somehow been fooled? He wouldn't put that past Kylo Ren. And he trusted Rey. If she said Chewbacca was alive, he was alive.

But that might not matter. Because they were all about to die.

Finn couldn't conceive another outcome. TIE fighter after TIE fighter sped out of the Star Destroyer to swarm the sky above Kijimi City. Zorii might have shown them how to elude the troopers and urban assault walkers on their way to Ochi's ship, but they'd never able to elude so many TIEs, especially when Poe told Finn *not* to get in the turret.

"You don't think I can hit any?" Finn asked as he ran up the ramp of the *Bestoon Legacy*. Poe had parked the ship in the repair field of a mechanic he knew.

"I'm thinking we can't take that chance," Poe said. He ushered the last of their group—C-3PO—inside and then closed the hatch. "If you do hit any, our cover's blown."

"Cover?"

Poe left Finn's question hanging as he hurried to the cockpit. Finn and the droids went with him. Rey had already sat herself in the pilot's seat. Poe took the copilot's station and switched on the engines, forgoing any warm-up procedures. "Hang tight, we're going up hot!"

Finn grabbed a handhold and the ship blasted off the ground. The sandy floor interfered with the droids' magnetic locks and they tumbled into the bulkhead. Finn nearly fell over himself when he saw their trajectory—they were heading straight toward the Star Destroyer.

What was Poe thinking? And why wasn't Rey doing anything about it?

Poe inserted a device into a slot on the control panel. Lights flashed from red to green, and then there was a chime. "Medallion works," he said. "Cleared for cargo hangar twelve."

A squadron of TIE fighters coming to attack veered away. The others gave them a wide berth, and the *Bestoon Legacy* joined a stream of traffic flying in and out of the *Steadfast*.

"Chewie, we're coming," Rey said.

Poe explained that the captain's medallion Zorii had given him granted them the highest clearance levels as a supply ship for the First Order fleet. And that seemed to be the case. They landed in cargo hangar twelve of the Destroyer without being harassed or contacted.

Such a security hole seemed insane, but Finn took this as another sign of the First Order's arrogance. They were so assured of their own military might that, even after the disaster that befell Starkiller Base, they couldn't imagine a single ship causing any major damage.

The medallion didn't curb all security measures. Two stormtroopers came over to the ship when the ramp lowered. "Credentials and manifest—"

The trooper didn't finish his sentence, stunned by Finn's blast. Poe silenced the other one with a shot. They hastened down the ramp with Rey while the droids stayed behind on the ship. Finn would've suggested they steal the troopers' armor, but they didn't have time to change.

"Which way?" Poe asked.

Finn looked around. The *Steadfast* had a slightly different layout than the *Finalizer* and the other Star Destroyers on which he'd served. The hangar itself was huge and contained a number of supply ships unloading cargo. "No idea," he said before spotting a corridor that on the *Finalizer* would have led to the detention area. His instincts told him it would be the same on the *Steadfast*. "Follow me."

Poe and Rey hurried into the passage after him. It was hard to check if they were heading in the right direction. There weren't any directories posted, and they'd have to hack into a terminal to access the schematics. As handy as it was, the medallion couldn't help with that.

Their biggest problem was that they were dressed in plain clothes and looked like they didn't belong on a First Order Destroyer. This was most apparent when they bumped into two stormtroopers rounding a corner. The pair immediately lifted their rifles. "Drop your weapons!" one ordered.

Finn realized he'd be shot if he even twitched the wrong way. But then Rey did something out of the ordinary. "It's okay that we're here," she told the troopers, waving her hand.

The troopers stared at them for a moment. At first, Finn thought they were as confused as he was that an intruder would dare say something so blatantly false. But then the lead trooper repeated what Rey had said. "It's okay that you're here."

His partner backed him up. "Thank goodness you're here." Both troopers lowered their rifles.

The Jedi of old supposedly had powers of persuasion—Jedi mind tricks, they were called. Like most rational people, Finn had never taken those stories seriously until he had witnessed what Rey could do. She had made him a believer.

Poe leaned over to Finn. "Does she do that to us?"

Finn knew Poe was joking and that Rey wouldn't use a mind trick on any of her friends. What was worrisome was if someone who lacked Rey's principles wielded such powers. Was that what had happened with the First Order? Had Finn's own mind, and the minds of all the children taken to be soldiers, been somehow warped and influenced by a dark power?

"We're looking for a prisoner," Rey said to the troopers, waving her hand again. "Tall, hairy, nasty temper. Had some belongings."

"You mean the Wookiee?" The lead trooper looked at his partner. "Eff-Enn-Eight-Four-Eight-Nine, you brought one aboard."

"Barely," FN-8489 said. "The beast sent eight of our guys to the infirmary—and he had binders on."

"Where might he be detained?" Rey asked.

"Cell six of the detention block, past the blast door at the junction, that way." FN-8489 pointed his rifle down the passage. "Listen for the howl. Can't miss it."

The three heeded the troopers' advice and continued down the corridor, shooting at any security camera they noticed that could monitor them. When they came to the blast door, Finn overrode the controls with an old First Order code. The blast door whooshed open.

Finn and Poe headed into the detention block, but Rey didn't move. She looked down another corridor.

Finn tried to get her attention. "They said Chewie's this way."

"The dagger's on this ship," Rey said. "We need it."

"What? Why?" Poe asked.

"A feeling. I'll meet you back in the hangar." She raced down the other corridor.

"Rey, you just can't—" Finn was about to follow, but Poe held him back.

"Chewie," Poe reminded him.

Finn watched her disappear. "She thinks she can do it all, on her own. Doesn't listen to anyone, doesn't tell anyone what's going on. She keeps it all in."

"You're just realizing that now?" Poe said. He headed through the open doorway. "C'mon, before we run into more troopers—unless you also do Jedi mind tricks."

Only one officer was on duty in the detention block—yet another sign of the First Order's overconfidence. Finn distracted him while Poe switched off the security cameras and then subdued the officer with a stun bolt.

As FN-8489 had said, Chewbacca's howls led them to the interrogation cell. The badge taken from the duty officer opened the cell door.

Chewbacca lay in an exhausted heap on the floor, rocking back and forth. But when he lifted his head and saw them, his groaning subsided. He barked what sounded like a question. Poe understood some of the Shyriiwook language and answered. "Of course we came for you!"

Chewbacca ruffed a name even Finn recognized. "Yeah, Rey's with us," Finn said. "She went to get the dagger."

They assisted the Wookiee up and out of the cell. Chewbacca shook out his coat and had enough strength to keep up with them on his own.

The duty officer was still unconscious, so the three hastened out of the detention center without incident. They went back the way they'd come, blasters drawn, with Finn out front. "We've got Ochi's ship," he said to Chewie. "Follow me."

Coming into the junction, Finn crossed paths with a stormtrooper. Not a second was wasted on conversation. Finn fired at the trooper and turned back. "Wrong way."

The three hurried down the other corridor, only to run into more stormtroopers, who immediately began firing. "Not really a right way, is there?" Poe said.

Poe knocked down some of the troopers with his shots, then slid a stormtrooper rifle Chewbacca's way. The Wookiee picked it up and all three rushed down the passage, firing at any stormtroopers in their way.

"We close?" Poe asked.

"Straight ahead," Finn said.

The hangar was in view at the end of the corridor when a trooper yelled, "Halt!" A flurry of blaster bolts flew around them and one struck Poe in the arm. He dropped his pistol and fell.

Chewbacca took care of the trooper who had shot Poe while Finn rushed to his friend's side. "You okay?"

Poe winced, clutching his arm. He lifted his head as stormtrooper squads converged on them. "Nope," he said.

"You there, hands up, drop your weapons," a trooper ordered. "Now!"

Reluctantly, the three did as commanded. There was no chance they could shoot their way out of this one. They were completely outmanned and outgunned.

Finn had been right about what he'd feared in the cockpit of Ochi's ship; he'd just picked the wrong moment.

They were all about to die.

CHAPTER 13

REY HAD SAID she'd sensed Ochi's dagger was on the Star Destroyer. But there was more to it than that. The dark side tugged at her. And as on Ahch-To, she couldn't resist following it.

It drew her through the corridors of the *Steadfast*, where she snuck past stormtroopers and officers. It took her up one lift, down another, through engineering, and near the barracks. It led her to a sparsely furnished white room that could only be the private quarters of Kylo Ren.

On an obsidian pedestal sat a relic far more terrifying than any Sith dagger—a helmet and mask that for a generation had been the face of ultimate evil in the galaxy.

Ravaged by fire, what remained made a most hideous form. No longer a polished and glistening black, the durasteel had dulled to the ghastly gray of ash. The mask's triangular grill, notorious for the breath that had rasped out of it, had become a jagged maw. And stripped of their lenses, the eyeholes were dark and soulless, just like the monster who had once stared through them.

This charred relic was all that was left of the Dark Lord

of the Sith, Darth Vader. Despite his death decades earlier, this remnant of his terror still simmered with pain, loneliness, and hate. Rey forced herself to look away.

On a shelf opposite the pedestal lay Chewbacca's bowcaster. Next to it was his bandolier, shoulder satchel, and the dagger of Ochi of Bestoon.

Rey picked up the dagger and the bandolier, then put the bandolier back down. The dagger took all her attention.

Its handle was cold to the touch, so cold she shivered. She heard the echo of screams. A woman, a man. A child. The sounds reverberated from the metal of the blade.

"Rey," said a voice.

Rey grabbed her lightsaber with her free hand and activated it. What she saw with her eyes was not what she saw in her mind. Her eyes saw the rest of the room. Her mind saw Kylo Ren.

"Wherever you are, you are hard to find," he said. The voice he projected was the one modulated by his mask, lower in tone, with the crackle of static electricity.

"You're hard to get rid of," she replied, and turned her mind away from his.

"I pushed you in the desert because I needed to see it. I needed you to see it—who you really are," Ren said. "I know the rest of your story, Rey."

Those words were perhaps the only ones that could make her mind tune back to him. He might not be in the room, but she pointed her saber at him.

"You're lying," she said, hoping he was.

"I've never lied to you," he said. "Your parents were no one. They chose to keep you safe."

She hissed to shush him. He kept talking. "You remember more than you say. I've been in your head."

"I don't want this!" she cried out.

"Search your memory," Ren said.

She was done with their conversation. Whatever new truths he could tell her would only further confuse her and hurt her. Kylo Ren used truth as a weapon.

Rey used her lightsaber as hers.

She swung her blade at him, as if he were actually there and not a vision in her mind. Ren lit his red saber and raised it to parry. The sabers sizzled against each other—as if they were in the same space.

"Remember them," Ren said. "Hear them. See them."

She couldn't resist any longer. She listened. She looked. She remembered.

Rey returned to the memory from her vision in the jungle. She was a young girl, clutched in a tight embrace by a young woman in a blue shawl. They were in a tent that smelled of Jakku. The woman's shawl fell back, and Rey saw the woman's face. Her mother's face. She was crying.

"Rey, be brave," her mother said. She wouldn't let Rey go. Rey wouldn't let her go, either.

A young man ducked into the tent. He had the scruff of a red beard. Sad blue eyes. He touched Rey's cheeks. A father's touch. "You'll be safe here," he said. "I promise."

His eyes flamed into the two rear thrusters of Ochi's

transport. Rey screamed, trying to free herself from Unkar Plutt's grip as she watched the ship rocket off Jakku.

Rey pulled away from the memory. She also pulled apart their lightsabers, propelling Ren back. But Ren was undeterred. "They sold you to protect you—"

"Stop talking!"

"Rey, I know what happened to them—"

She lunged at him. Ren blocked her attack but took a step back. And then her saber blade connected, spilling something red onto the floor of the room. A glance revealed she hadn't drawn blood. Red berries rolled about her feet, berries that looked remarkably similar to the ones she had eaten in Babu Frik's workshop. Kylo Ren must be down on Kijimi.

She and Ren circled each other like predators. "You don't know the whole story," he said. "Tell me where you are."

That she would never do. He continued to push at her. "It was Palpatine who had your parents taken. He was looking for you," Ren said. "But they wouldn't say where you were. So he gave the order."

A scene flashed in her mind. She saw the puckered face of Ochi of Bestoon as he stood in the passenger compartment of his transport, holding out his dagger at Rey's parents. "She isn't on Jakku. She's gone," her mother said. Her lie was unacceptable to Ochi. He did the bidding of his master and stabbed Rey's father and then her mother to death.

Rey broke away from the scene and flew at Ren, furious and fierce, slashing her saber over him and under him. He backpedaled and parried in all directions, on the defensive.

One of her swings was too broad, and she cleaved the pedestal in half. The helmet and mask of Darth Vader tumbled to the floor—and disappeared.

Ren glanced at his feet, as if something had landed there. He looked back at Rey. "So that's where you are."

She used the opportunity to attack again. He brought his saber up and they crossed blades, their faces—their presences—close to each other. "Do you know why the Emperor's always wanted you dead?" Ren asked.

Rey pushed her blade more into his. The edge of hers sizzled near Ren's cracked helmet.

"I'll come tell you," he said, and was gone.

Rey stood in the room, alone. She extinguished her blade and caught her breath. The smashed black bits of the pedestal lay scattered on the floor, among the red berries.

What had she been thinking, entering the quarters of the First Order's Supreme Leader? If Ren had deduced she was there, it would be mere moments before he called the forces on the Destroyer to apprehend her and her friends.

That was what the dark side did. It lured its victims into traps from which they could not escape.

She slipped the dagger through her belt, grabbed her staff and Chewie's belongings, and ran out of Ren's quarters.

Finn faced a wall, arms behind him. Poe and Chewbacca stood to either side of him, doing the same.

"Terminate them," Allegiant General Pryde, the *Steadfast*'s captain, had said before handing them over to General Hux and a stormtrooper squad to do the deed.

Each and every sound Finn heard gave him a count-down to his death. Boots clacked on the floor behind him as the firing squad took up position. Blaster safeties were unsnapped. Armor plates jiggled when rifles were raised. Finn didn't dare look at Poe or Chewie. He didn't want the last thing he saw to be the anguish on their faces.

General Hux interceded before triggers were pulled. "I'd like to do this one myself," he said.

The reprieve brought Finn no comfort. He'd rather die at the hands of his former partners-in-arms than be shot by that sniveling coward of a general.

In the brief seconds they had left, Poe turned his head to Finn. "What were you going to tell Rey? In the tunnels."

"You still on that?" Finn asked him.

Blaster bolts rang out and Finn shut his eyes. When he heard the thud of bodies that weren't his own, he peeked over at his friends. Poe and Chewbacca were still standing, still breathing, still alive. Finn spun around with them.

The three stormtroopers of the firing squad lay sprawled at General Hux's feet, with blaster-bolt-sized holes in their armor. Hux motioned with the offending blaster rifle. "We don't have much time," he said.

Poe's question echoed Finn's own confusion. "What?"

"I'm the spy," Hux said.

Finn blinked. *"You?"* But it made sense. Only someone as high up in the First Order as Hux would have access to the confidential data on Exegol and the Sith fleet given to Boolio.

Poe pointed at the general and smiled. "I knew it!"

Finn shook his head. "No, you did not—"

"Let's go," Hux said.

He fled the chamber, leaving Finn, Poe, and Chewbacca no choice but to follow.

"Look! There they are!" said a haughty electronic voice.

Finn looked down a side passage, where C-3PO, BB-8, and Ochi's droid hurried toward them. Chewbacca's bandolier hung across C-3PO's chest and he hefted the bowcaster and satchel in his metal arms. Finn thought the droids were on Ochi's ship. How had they found Chewie's belongings?

Poe wasn't waiting for explanations. "Come on!" he shouted to the droids.

Hux halted at a blast door. "After I shut down the impeders, you've got seconds."

This was all going so fast and Finn had so many questions. Seconds for what? Why was General Hux, of all people, helping them?

The blast door opened and Finn smelled engine fuel. In the hangar beyond sat the *Millennium Falcon*.

"There she is," Poe said. "She's a survivor."

He ran right toward the *Falcon*, with Chewbacca and the droids going after him. General Hux grabbed Finn. "Wait!"

Hux placed the blaster rifle in Finn's hands. "Blast me in the arm—quick!"

Finn aimed the rifle at Hux. But he didn't shoot. This all seemed too wacky. Why was the former commander of Starkiller Base aiding Finn's team escape? Had General Armitage Hux, who had developed the brainwashing methods to instill complete loyalty to the First Order, actually turned traitor to the First Order?

"Do it so they don't know what I did!" Hux implored.

Finn fired a glancing shot at Hux's leg, ensuring that Hux couldn't try to run away and betray them. The general bit his lip, stifling a cry from a bad blaster burn. Perhaps he wasn't as much of a coward as Finn thought he was.

"Why are you helping us?" Finn asked.

Hux arched his upper lip. "I don't care if you win." He rocked back and forth, holding his leg. "I need Kylo Ren to lose."

Finn asked no more questions. That answer was good enough.

Kylo Ren was not going to lose. Not this time.

He landed in the *Steadfast*, having made the short trip from Kijimi's surface in a TIE whisper. Ren opened the hatch and strode down the ramp alone.

The scavenger girl stood in the center of the hangar, her hand near the hilt of the lightsaber on her belt. That sword made him sick. It had once been the property of Luke and Anakin Skywalker—the Anakin who was a Jedi Knight and had not yet made himself into Darth Vader. Though the hilt had split during Ren's battle with Rey on the *Supremacy*, it seemed that she had found a way to repair it.

Ren let his hands hang free under his cloak. He wouldn't need his lightsaber in this fight. The truths he had learned on Exegol would hurt her more than his blade ever could.

Squads of stormtroopers rushed from all corridors into the bay. They halted when they saw him approaching the girl. He would take care of Rey himself.

He moved as she moved, like they were two stars sharing the same orbit. She stopped before the hangar's entrance, the only place where stormtrooper rifles weren't pointed at her back. He also stopped and waited. It was her time to speak.

"Why did the Emperor come for me?" she asked. "Why did he want to kill a child? Tell me."

"Because he saw what you would become," Ren said. "You don't just have power. You have his power. You're his granddaughter. You are a Palpatine."

She shuddered but did not seem otherwise shocked. He did not expect her to be. There were secrets in that mind of hers that she had tried to bury and forget. But the truth could not be buried. It could not be forgotten. And the quicker she accepted it, the quicker she could realize her full potential.

"My mother was the daughter of Vader. Your father was the son of the Emperor," he said, stepping toward her as she stepped backward. "What Palpatine doesn't know is that we're a dyad in the Force, Rey. Two that are one. We'll kill him together and take the throne."

She went to the edge of the hangar. The magnetic containment field had been turned off since they were in atmosphere, and Kijimi's wind blew her hair. She peered down, as if contemplating a jump, then looked back at him.

He removed his helmet and mask to draw her focus back to him. He wanted her to see his truth, that he wasn't Ben Solo hiding under a mask as she believed, but that he had accepted himself as Kylo Ren.

"You know what you need to do," he said, his voice raw and unmodulated. "You know."

As he had once before, Ren extended his hand toward her. She stared at it, her own hands clenched but shaking. Her eyes moved to the scar on his face, the scar she had given him in their first duel. She was trembling, and he could feel her weaken, teetering between acceptance and defiance.

He waited for her again, to acknowledge the truth of who she was.

"I do," she finally said.

With a deafening roar, the *Millennium Falcon* rose in the portal behind her.

The stormtrooper squads had a target. They opened fire on the *Falcon*, their blasters hitting vital components. Flames burst on the freighter's hull. Smoke and steam billowed from pipes.

The *Falcon* spun around so the engine thruster banks faced the portal. The thrusters blazed at full burn, blasting a superheated wind into the hangar. Cargo crates, stormtroopers, and even some supply ships were yanked into the air and out of the hangar.

Ren planted his feet on the floor and anchored himself in the Force as everything else whirled around him.

In that brief time, the *Falcon*'s landing ramp extended and the renegade stormtrooper FN-2187 emerged, a breathing mask over his mouth and nose. He fired at the few stormtroopers who still stood. "Rey, come on!" he called.

She looked at him, then back at Ren.

Ren kept his hand held out to her. She could not turn away from who she was now.

Rey leapt onto the ramp and ran aboard the *Falcon*, never glancing back. The renegade trooper shot a look at Ren, and then the hatch closed. Ren watched the freighter disappear into the dark of the Kijimi night.

She had made her choice. She chose defiance.

He did not order pursuit. He knew where they were going.

They weren't the only ones who could translate the runes on Ochi's dagger.

CHAPTER 14

FINN ENTERED the lounge to find Rey reaching into an upper access panel, making repairs. The stormtroopers' blasters had done a number on the *Millennium Falcon's* exposed componentry. Miraculously, what hadn't been damaged was the *Falcon's* notoriously faulty hyperdrive. For once it worked flawlessly, lightspeeding them away from Kijimi to the coordinates that C-3PO translated from the runes. During the hyperspace journey, the crew hurried to make emergency repairs so that when the *Falcon* emerged from lightspeed, it wasn't a smoking wreck. They were in such a rush Poe had only applied basic first aid to his blaster wound.

But Finn was less worried about the state of the *Falcon* than he was about the state of his friend.

He walked over and helped Rey with the repairs. After a few minutes of tightening tribolts, he told her what was on his mind. "You can't trust what Ren said."

Sparks flew as she fused a frayed connection. "All that matters is the wayfinder. Getting to Exegol."

"That's what we're doing," he said.

"Not you. *Me*." Rey looked off, as if struck by something. "He killed my mother and my father. I'm going to find Palpatine—and *I'm* going to destroy him."

The Rey whom Finn had befriended had always been stubborn and a loner, but never someone bent on revenge. "Rey, that doesn't sound like you. I know you—"

"People keep telling me they know me." She pressed the panel closed. "I'm afraid no one does."

Rey left the lounge without a glance back. Finn grew even more worried.

After the droids in the infirmary wrapped a bacta bandage around his leg and discharged him to rest in his quarters, General Armitage Hux went straight to the bridge.

Every step was painful, yet each one reminded him he was closer to his crowning achievement, the fulfillment of a dream he'd nurtured for as long as he could remember.

Friendless as a boy, and never knowing his mother, Hux had found comfort and strength in his father's stories of the glorious Empire that had brought order to the galaxy after the chaos of the Clone Wars. Yet as proud as Brendol Hux was of his own Imperial service, he had no such pride in his son. He'd say that Armitage would never make anything of himself. He was stupid. He was weak. He didn't have a spine. And then Armitage would endure a slap that turned into a smack that often became a pummeling.

Rey trains in the Force under the guidance of Leia Organa but is still testing the limits of her abilities.

The Trodatome named Klaud accompanies Chewbacca, Poe Dameron, and Finn on a mission to the Sinta Glacier Colony.

General Hux has accepted Kylo Ren as Supreme Leader of the First Order . . . or has he?

Finn takes the gunner's seat as the *Falcon* is pursued by First Order TIE fighters!

R2-D2 and C-3PO: best friends forever

Finn, Rose Tico, and Poe are three of the Resistance's most dedicated heroes.

Rey's friends accompany her to the planet Pasaana as they search for the path to Exegol.

The Knights of Ren follow the Resistance heroes to Pasaana.

Lando Calrissian is a hero of the Rebellion against the Empire who helped destroy the second Death Star.

Sometimes a friend needs a lift! Chewie lends BB-8 a hand.

Zorii Bliss is an old friend—or is it enemy?—of Poe Dameron's.

Babu Frik may be tiny, but he is the best there is at droid repair. Poe seeks him out to help C-3PO decipher engravings in the Sith language.

C-3PO is able to translate the Sith writing with help from Babu Frik . . . but the task completely wipes his memory.

Rey and Kylo Ren have a showdown on Kijimi.

Kylo Ren uses a Sith wayfinder to make his way to
Exegol, where he discovers Emperor Palpatine.

Jannah was trained to be a First Order stormtrooper, but like Finn, she could not obey their terrible orders and escaped.

BB-8 finds a new friend, D-O, on the assassin Ochi's abandoned ship.

Jannah holds Finn back
when he tries to help Rey
as she faces off against
Kylo Ren on Kef Bir.

Red Sith troopers patrol
the corridors of the
new Sith Star Destroyers.

Rey and Kylo Ren face off in an epic lightsaber battle!

Hux promised himself at an early age he would show how wrong his father was about him. If a senator from Naboo could rise from obscurity to lead the greatest military power the galaxy had ever seen and become Emperor, he could do the same. He could be the one to bring order to the chaos sown by the New Republic. He could be the savior—and ruler—of the galaxy.

His ability more than matched his ambition. He had quickly risen through the First Order's ranks to become its youngest general, championing advanced weapons programs like Starkiller Base, the orbital autocannons, and the portable superlasers that had yet to be deployed. He also overhauled the stormtrooper training program that his father had begun. Hux's new methods stressed loyalty to the First Order above everything else. Aside from a few anomalies like FN-2187 and the mutinous Company 77, the system produced stormtroopers whose extreme loyalty encouraged their lethality, since they experienced no guilt for what they were charged to do.

These accomplishments won Hux the favor of the former Supreme Leader, and the rank and file soon viewed him as Snoke's logical successor. No one was more loyal to the vision of the First Order than General Armitage Hux.

Then came Kylo Ren.

Riding the lift to the bridge, Hux bristled at the very thought of his nemesis. Ren had no military training and held no actual rank, yet Snoke had taken him under his wing and taught him his infernal powers. The dark side, Snoke had called it. With those powers, Ren had been transformed into a one-man Starkiller, terrifying the galaxy at large.

Hux had made a grave mistake overestimating Snoke's sway over the young man and underestimating Ren's powers. Hux had thought Ren too volatile, too involved in his own maniacal pursuits to try to take command of the First Order. But then Ren had done just that, murdering his master and assuming the role of Supreme Leader. Now he was turning the First Order into his personal combat force to carry out his bidding for whatever crusade he was on.

Strange then, Hux mused as the lift stopped and its doors opened, that his greatest act of loyalty to the First Order would be to betray it. But better he do that than let Ren destroy everything he had worked so hard to build.

For just as Hux had taken revenge on his father by arranging his poisoning, he would also have his revenge on Kylo Ren.

Exiting the lift, Hux crossed the bridge. Allegiant General Pryde stood before an expansive viewport, hands behind his back, staring at the stars. "What happened?" he asked when Hux came up behind him. There was no concern in his voice.

Hux didn't expect Pryde to be sympathetic. The animosity between them was mutual. "It was a coordinated incursion. They overpowered the guards and forced me to take them to their ship."

Pryde's face wrinkled in concern. Even if he saw

through Hux's lie, Hux was confident there was little Pryde could do to retaliate against him. Pryde was respected only because of his closeness to Kylo Ren. During the war with the Resistance, Pryde had stayed conveniently far from the front lines. Ren had only awarded him the rank of allegiant general as a way to mock Hux. And all the officers and stormtroopers on the bridge knew it.

Pryde addressed a lieutenant. "Get me the Supreme Leader."

Hux had primed himself for this moment. When Kylo Ren's hologram shimmered before him, he would accuse Ren of betraying the First Order. He would say that Ren was the one who had supplied the Resistance with information about the new fleet in the Unknown Regions. Since Ren had left the *Steadfast* on another of his lunatic quests, the officers and troops would be outside the orbit of his dark influence. They would rally to Hux. And he would finally become the Supreme Leader he deserved to be.

Pryde didn't wait for Ren to answer the comm. He snatched a blaster rifle from a stormtrooper and pointed it at Hux. Hux had no time to react. Neither did anyone else on the bridge. Pryde pulled the trigger and Hux crumpled to the bridge floor, shot in the chest.

"Tell him we found our spy," Pryde told the lieutenant.

Sound faded, then light, then pain, and finally Hux's last hold on life and his dream.

CHAPTER 15

REY FIXED the compressor, but that wasn't enough. The *Millennium Falcon* came out of hyperspace into the Endor system a smoking wreck.

At the *Falcon*'s helm, Poe and Chewbacca avoided any collisions with the gas giant of Endor and the numerous satellites that circled it, which was no small feat for a ship with busted engines. They even managed to stay out of detection range of the First Order Star Destroyer that guarded the system. But once they reached the moon Kef Bir, a rough weather pattern sent the *Falcon* in an uncontrollable descent. Repairs to the landing gear and its repulsors hadn't been completed, so there was no way to cushion a hard landing. A full-on crash was only averted when Poe pulled back on the yoke and skidded the *Falcon* for kilometers along a grassy plain, leaving a deep gouge behind it.

Rey wasn't pleased, though admittedly she couldn't have done any better. But with their small crew, it would take days, maybe even weeks, to make the *Falcon* spaceworthy again. And that was only if they could get the right parts—which would be impossible on a moon that was, according to scouting reports, devoid of settlements.

They might be stranded on Kef Bir for a long time.

Poe wanted to start repairs with whatever they had, but Rey argued they needed to find the wayfinder first. She led the droids, Finn, Chewbacca, and a reluctant Poe out of the *Falcon* and across the grasslands.

They hadn't walked far when they ascended a hill and came to the edge of a cliff. Beyond them tossed a mighty ocean that vanished in a dense stormy haze. Spray hit their faces from huge tidal waves pounding against the cliff.

Rey stood in awe of the endless swell of water. She'd seen the ocean on Ahch-To, but it hadn't roiled with such raw violence.

The haze in the background broke, disclosing an even more incredible sight. A mountain of curved and jagged metal protruded from the waves in the distance.

"What-what-what is that?" D-O asked.

"The Death Star," Rey said. "A bad place from an old war."

The Empire's second battle station had orbited Endor thirty years earlier as an artificial moon. It had still been under construction when the Rebel Alliance took the majority of their forces there in a last-ditch attack to defeat the Empire. The *Millennium Falcon*, flown by Lando Calrissian and Nien Nunb, a Sullustan pilot Rey had met in the Resistance, headed the squadron that destroyed the Death Star.

BB-8 beeped, asking where it came from. "From the sky," Rey said, knowing destruction was never total. As with all things that exploded, there was debris. And this chunk of the battle station had plunged into the oceans of Kef Bir, causing untold damage to the moon.

Finn mused aloud what the Sith runes had said. "The wayfinder's in the Imperial vault . . . in the Death Star."

Poe surveyed the view. "I hate to be practical, but it's going to take years to find it."

"Oh dear," C-3PO said.

Rey stared at the sharp and serrated chunks of the Death Star. One jutting beam called to mind a similar shape. "Only this blade tells. . . ."

She took Ochi's dagger from her satchel and examined it. Something poked from the crossguard of the hilt. She wiggled it and pulled out a slim, arc-shaped extension.

An idea came to her. She held up the dagger, placing it on the same eyeline as the jutting Death Star beam. The double arrowheads of the blade fit into the contours of the wreckage like a puzzle piece. The arc-shaped extension worked like a direction guide on a compass, pointing at a collapsed tower.

"The wayfinder's there," Rey said.

Hoofbeats rattled the ground, and someone shouted over the crash of waves. "Rough landing!"

Rey turned around. Eleven riders on tusked, woolly quadrupeds crested the hillside. Many had mechanized bows with quivers hanging from their saddles. Their leader was a human female in her twenties, with dark brown eyes and curly black hair. Her tunic was made from animal hides, and her cape was cut from a survival blanket. Across her forehead she wore a banded pair of macrobinoculars and around her waist a utility belt.

Poe lifted his pistol. "I've seen worse."

The woman was not at all intimidated. She glanced back at the trench dug by the *Falcon*'s landing. "I've seen better. Are you Resistance?"

"Depends," Poe said.

She gave the group a hard look, as if trying to suss out their loyalties. "We picked up a transmission from someone named Babu Frik."

The name had an immediate effect on the group. Poe lowered his pistol while C-3PO waved his arms. "Babu Frik!" the droid exclaimed. "He's one of my oldest friends!"

"He said you were the last hope."

The gravity of that muted C-3PO's excitement. Rey had heard such grand pronouncements before; she had even made one when trying to convince Luke Skywalker to leave Ahch-To and join the Resistance.

But grand pronouncements weren't beneficial to the task at hand. Rey pointed at the half-submerged Death Star. "We need to get out to that wreck. There's something inside there we need."

"Something that could end the war for good," Poe added.

The woman looked to the other riders. They gave her discreet nods. "I can take you out there by skimmer."

Finn was watching fifty-meter-tall waves smash against the wreckage. "Do you see that water?"

"Too dangerous now," the woman said. "We can get there at low tide. First light tomorrow."

Rey felt a dark presence approaching in the distance. "We can't wait that long. Kylo Ren's right behind us."

The leader of the riders sat up in her saddle. *"Kylo Ren?"*

"We don't have time." Gripping the dagger hilt, Rey turned back to the Death Star.

Poe holstered his blaster. "For my choice, let's fix the ship." He looked up at the woman. "Do you have parts?

"Some. I'm Jannah." She pulled the reins of her steed and started down the other side of the slope with her riders. Poe, Chewbacca, and the droids followed her.

Rey did not move from her position on the cliff. The Death Star tugged at her just as the dagger on the Star Destroyer and the geyser hole on Ahch-To had.

She heard Finn behind her. She could feel his eyes on her back. He was still concerned about her.

But after a few moments, he left her alone.

Finn knew Kylo Ren might be coming, but the main priority occupying everyone's attention was fixing the *Falcon*—and it required a team effort.

While BB-8 and D-O stood watch outside the *Falcon* and amused the orbaks—what the riders called their shaggy four-legged mounts—Jannah's company hammered new armor plates to the hull. In the cockpit, Poe and Chewbacca messed with circuitry and ordered C-3PO on simple errands, fetching hydrospanners, Harris wrenches, and spacer's tape. Back to his old self, C-3PO commented how absurd it was for a protocol droid to be doing starship maintenance.

"Do we know where his mute switch is?" Finn heard Poe ask Chewie. The Wookiee laughed, and C-3PO departed the cockpit in a huff.

"I'm fluent in over four million forms of communication, and this is what they want me to do?" the droid said, clinking past Finn. "If my maker even knew!"

On his hands and knees in the *Falcon*'s main corridor, Finn almost questioned the droid. Wasn't he always boasting about being fluent in *seven* million forms of communication? Babu's memory wipe must have wiped out that fact, too. But Finn kept it to himself, because if he corrected the droid, C-3PO might never stop talking to him—and then Finn might never get around to finishing his repairs.

From the way it was going, that might not happen anyway.

Finn had volunteered to work on the *Falcon*'s landing gear but discovered that although he could see what to fix, he might not be able to do it without an intact rez plate.

Fortunately, that was exactly what Jannah brought him from her supplies. "It's an oh-six, but it'll work."

The code on the rez plate's identification label surprised Finn. "That's a First Order part."

Jannah nodded. "There's an old cruiser on the west ridge, which we stripped for parts."

"The First Order landed a ship here?" Finn asked. He'd heard that when the New Republic was in power, it had placed a strict security cordon around Endor.

"It's the ship we were assigned to," Jannah said. "The one we escaped in."

Finn looked up at the young woman. He had neglected to notice that most of what she wore was First Order–issue—the macrobinoculars, the survival tarp repurposed as a cape, an armor plate wrapped around her arm that doubled as a transponder. "You were First Order?"

"Not by choice. Conscripted as kids. All of us." Her tough veneer softened, revealing someone who was more than just a soldier. "I was Tee-Zed-One-Seven-One-Nine. Stormtrooper. Of Company Seventy-Seven."

"Eff-Enn-Two-One-Eight-Seven," Finn said. He'd been called that much of his life, but now that designation sounded like someone else's name.

She leaned closer to him. "You?"

BB-8 zoomed past them into the cockpit, beeping up a storm. Relieved by the interruption, Finn opened up the gear drum and examined where the rez plate should go.

Jannah filled in the silence. "We mutinied at the Battle of Ansett Island. They told us to fire on civilians. We wouldn't do it. We laid down our weapons."

Banging echoed through the hull from Jannah's comrades. "All of you?" Finn asked.

"The whole company. I don't even know how it happened. Wasn't even a decision, really. More like—"

"An instinct," Finn said. He slid the rez plate into the drum. It fit perfectly. "A feeling."

Jannah 's eyes widened in realization. "A feeling."

Finn closed the landing gear panel and stood. "The Force. It brought me here. Brought me to Rey and Poe."

"You say that like you're sure it's real," Jannah said.

"Oh, it's very real," Finn said. Throughout his youth, his First Order instructors had taught him that the Force was a myth and the feats of the Jedi mere parlor tricks. But seeing what Rey could do—and what they could all do together—revealed that much of what he'd been taught was a lie.

"I wasn't sure then," he told Jannah. "But I'm sure now."

BB-8 sped into the corridor, followed by Poe. "Rey's gone," the pilot said.

Finn was first out of the *Falcon*, with the others hurrying after him. He ran up the hill to the cliff's edge, staring out at the choppy sea. He saw nothing but its colossal swells.

"She took the skimmer," Jannah said.

Poe looked through his quadnocs. They hummed as he adjusted magnification. "She's out there, heading toward the Death Star. Her skimmer keeps tipping over—it's damaged. What the heck is she thinking?"

Finn spied a dark speck far in the distance. A wave crashed and washed it from view. "We gotta go after her."

Poe lowered the quadnocs. "We'll fix the *Falcon* and get out there as fast as we can."

Finn spun on him. "We're going to lose her!"

Poe shrugged. "What do you want us to do? *She* left us."

"She's not herself," Finn said. "You don't know what she's fighting!"

"Oh, but you do?"

"I do." Finn glared at Poe. "And Leia does."

"I'm not Leia," Poe said. He started to turn away.

"That's for sure." Finn grabbed Poe's quadnocs. Poe let Finn have them and walked down the hill. The others followed him, except Jannah.

Finn found Rey's sea skimmer in the quadnocs. It bounced over the surf, one repulsor smoking, the other one barely pushing the skimmer above the water. To maneuver through the turmoil, Rey manipulated the skimmer's rudders and pulled a winch, swinging the outrigger over her head. It would smash into the water on the other side and stabilize the craft until another wave forced her to do it again. But hopscotching wasn't going to work in the giant waves near the Death Star. She'd need both engines to push her through or her skimmer would add to the wreckage.

"Finn," Jannah said, "there's another skimmer."

Finn lowered the quadnocs and looked out to the ocean. He could no longer see Rey or her skimmer without the enhanced magnification. But he did spot a claw-winged craft emerging from the dark clouds.

He didn't need the quadnocs to know what it was and who flew it. Kylo Ren's TIE fighter descended toward the Death Star.

CHAPTER 16

REY WAS DROWNING.

Her stubbornness had placed her in mortal peril again. She had stolen one of Jannah's sea skimmers from the shore and ventured out into the ocean alone. She had experience helming skiffs in Jakku's sandstorms, but she had scant experience swimming. And when a wall of water crashed down on her skimmer, splitting it apart and driving her into the depths, that was what she was forced to do.

She tumbled over herself, flailing her limbs, caught in an undertow. Water rushed into her nose and filled her lungs. Kef Bir was going to be her grave. The desert scavenger would be drowned on an ocean moon.

But she was more than that, more than a desert scavenger. She had trained under two of the greatest Jedi. What they had taught her could save her if she let go of the panic—if she relied on the Force.

She extended her arms and legs, reaching out to the tremendous natural power around her. The water churned with opposing currents, some from breaking waves, others from waves beginning to form. She found one of the rising currents and kicked into it. What the ocean could swallow, the ocean could also spit out.

The current dragged her up toward the surface and she burst out of the water. She floated on the crest of another wave as it was about to crash on a ruined section of the Death Star.

She paddled to the edge of the crest. As the wave broke, she rode that energy to fling herself into the air. Just as she couldn't swim, she couldn't fly. But it was never the falling that killed someone, it was the impact of the fall.

Rey called on the Force to slow her descent.

She landed on a deck of the Death Star with a jarring thump. Her ears popped and she hacked up water. A coughing fit seized her until she finally wheezed a breath. She rolled around to see another wave rise above her, seconds from breaking. She pushed herself up and staggered into a run. She found a turret pylon and wrapped her arms around it right as the wave smashed into the deck.

After the water washed away, Rey was still standing, hugging the pylon. She peered down to see the path she needed to take, indicated by the dagger's crossguard. In that hole the dark side whispered to her to come.

She closed her mind to those whispers but obeyed all the same, carefully sliding down the splintered hull. The terrain was treacherous inside, with sharp metal shafts and chasms severing corridors. But Rey had grown up traversing the interiors of crashed starships on Jakku, so she was innately familiar with this environment. She climbed, leapt, and crawled through the wreckage, every so often letting herself hear those whispers to guide her way.

When she scaled a turbolift shaft and emerged in a chamber with a high-backed chair before a shattered viewport, she knew she had entered the Emperor's throne room.

Rey moved closer until the deck plate beneath her broke under her weight. Jumping back, she noticed a spoke handle on the wall. The spoke turned of its own accord, opening a set of hidden doors.

She walked through the doorway into a hallway, which she could only guess led to the Emperor's personal vault. The doors shut behind her.

Around her she saw fragments of herself. An arm. The side of her face. Her back. The hem of her capelet. All reflected in the broken mirrors that lined the walls.

She quickened her pace, wishing to leave as soon as she could. At the far end of the hallway, floating in the air above a pedestal, was a small pyramidal object, glowing green with a blinking red dot in the center. She needed no tug or pull to be drawn toward it. She wanted to hold the Emperor's wayfinder in her hands.

Rey stopped before the pedestal and took the wayfinder. It was an old and fragile artifact, cold to the touch. Archaic runes and star chart symbols were inscribed in the black glass of the pyramid's sides. Once translated, they would reveal a route to the lost world of the Sith.

Exegol.

A dread came over her. Not of where she had to go, but of where she was. She was not alone in the hallway.

Rey turned. A figure in a dark cloak approached, brandishing a lightsaber with a bent hilt and two red blades. As the figure came into the light, cast from cracks in the walls, the mirrors reflected her face—and the shock on Rey's own.

The figure was her double, a Rey as pale and stark as Kylo Ren. Her double flicked a wrist and the lightsaber hilt straightened into a single piece, with the blades projecting out from both ends like a staff.

"Never be afraid of who you are," her double said, and attacked.

Rey lit her saber to ward off her double's blow. They crossed swords back and forth, dueling in the hallway. Rey tried to go on the offensive, but whenever she risked a thrust or a jab, her double mirrored her move, as if she already knew what Rey was going to do. Her double also had another advantage Rey could feel—a searing anger against Rey. In a frenzied blitz, her double pushed her to the vault doors and hissed like some infernal beast. The malign look on her double's face terrified Rey, for it was like seeing her own face twisted by evil. Rey stumbled backward through the doors, dropping the wayfinder.

She fell back into the throne room and her lightsaber deactivated. The wayfinder slid down the canted floor. When she jumped to her feet, her double was gone, but there was a new arrival.

Kylo Ren stood at the bottom of the slope, studying

the wayfinder he held in his black-gloved hand. "Two were made," he said, his face free of his mask. "One belongs to me, Vader's grandson."

He looked up at Rey. "This one belongs to you, heir to the power of the Sith."

She gathered her breath and stood, igniting her lightsaber again. Ren scoffed. "Look at yourself. You set out to find this wayfinder, to prove to my mother you're a Jedi. But you've proved something else. Who you really are." His gaze was penetrating. "You can't go back to her now. Like I can't."

"Give it to me," Rey said.

"The dark side is in our nature," he said. "Surrender to it."

"Give it . . . to me," she demanded.

"The only way you're getting to Exegol is with me." Ren squeezed the wayfinder. Corroded from the sea air, its sides shattered and its frame snapped. He flung the pieces away.

"No!" Rey screamed. She jumped and lashed out at him with her saber.

Ren dodged her swings, then activated his blade to parry. But that didn't stop her from continuing her assault. He was pushed out of the Emperor's throne room along a wide catwalk, on the defensive. Anger drove her attack—anger at him, at his destruction of the wayfinder, at the so-called truths he wouldn't stop telling her. If he refused to leave her alone, she would make him.

Their lightsabers clashed, plasma biting plasma. Waves crashed against the catwalk. Rain lashed down from storm clouds. Sometimes Ren disappeared, like a ghost, lost in fog and spray. Sometimes Rey felt herself disappear, lost in the fury of her assault. She felt stronger with every blow, while he seemed weakened, in constant retreat.

"Rey!"

The sound of her name stalled her momentum. She turned. Finn was sprinting toward her on the bridge, his hands cupping his mouth to shout again.

She swept out an arm and the Force hurled him backward. He landed far away on the bridge, the woman called Jannah running up beside him.

Rey turned back just as Ren tried to use the distraction to strike her down. Her blade met his and she renewed her attack, thrusting and stabbing at him with all her ferocity.

Ren continued backpedaling toward the end of the broken catwalk, where the ocean raged. Swells loomed over them. They batted blades, then Rey leapt away to avoid being pummeled by a crashing wave. Ren did the same.

Rey landed and charged at him. She'd never felt so alive, so focused, so invincible. Ren had made a mistake confronting her here. She was going to send him to a watery grave.

Ren blocked Rey's blade and reached out with his other hand. Opening his palm, he struck her with a wave of another kind—a wave of the Force.

She felt as if she had run right into a duracrete wall. Her breath was knocked out of her. Her bones rattled. She wobbled on her legs. But she did not fall back.

She raised her free hand and returned the blow. Her wave hit him square in the chest, shoving him backward. Yet he kept his footing.

Rey flew at him with her saber, swinging wildly. He matched her strokes, then assailed her with a surprising onslaught of his own. She was put on the defensive as he used his saber like a club, beating her backward. It was more than anger that fueled his surge; it was hate. She could feel it boiling off his blade. She fell, losing hold of her saber. It switched off and rolled away from her.

He loomed over her with his saber, and she knew she was done. But then he quit his attack. The fury vanished from his eyes. He stood there, stunned, and to Rey's disbelief, staggered back, dropping his weapon.

Leia Organa thanked Lieutenant Connix for assisting her to her quarters in the cave. Once there, she gently declined any further help, and Connix excused herself so Leia could sleep. Leia took her husband's medal off its peg, then sat on her bunk and laid down by herself.

Her eyes came to rest on a silver dome with a red indicator light and a thin memory slot. R2-D2 must have rolled into her quarters to check on her. She did not dismiss him. She recalled the time when she had inserted datatapes into his slot. It had been her most desperate hour, having to entrust secret plans to a random astromech droid. And that droid had outwitted an empire and delivered those plans into the right hands, setting in motion a chain of events that had changed the galaxy and her life.

R2-D2 wobbled forward and moaned softly, as if he knew what was to come. He murmured a farewell in binary that was not just from him but from his counterpart. As much as she adored C-3PO, she was glad he was not there. The golden droid would have fussed over her so much that she would never have found peace.

As her surroundings faded, the faces of her family came to her mind. Family she had lost. Her adoptive father and mother, Bail and Breha Organa. The brother she'd always known she had, Luke. Her mother, who had died during childbirth yet whose kindness had left such an impression that Leia had felt close to her throughout her life. Her father, who had done great evil and whose face she always associated with his black mask. She saw another face now, a man's face, lined with shame and remorse. Leia had never reconciled with Darth Vader, yet Luke had said he'd felt the good in him. Leia felt it now, too. This was not the time to erect more walls and cast blame. She accepted her father's apology and returned his love. The lines in his face lessened and his eyes lit up. He smiled.

And then there was Han, dear Han, scruffy-looking as ever, standing next to Chewie in the same grimy jacket he always seemed to wear, arms open for an embrace she'd never part from again. *I love you*, he said.

I know.

As those faces and memories also began to fade, Leia clasped the medal against her chest and thought of the person who had made her so happy since Han had gone. Han's last gift to her was bringing her a scavenger from Jakku who had become like an adopted daughter to Leia. Rey had so much spirit that merely imagining her sprinting through the jungle on one of her tests diminished some of Leia's pain. She would miss the girl—miss not enjoying a future with her—but she was happy to have spent the time with her she had. For all that Leia had endured, the Force had been good to her in the end. It had given her a second opportunity to be a mother. So many parents who lost their children never had that chance.

Last, she thought of the child she had lost.

Her son.

She missed and loved Ben, despite all he had done. She wondered if her grandmother had felt the same about Leia's father. A mother's love was unlike anything else in the universe. It was unbreakable. Eternal. Not even the dark side could rupture its bond.

She felt that Ben and Rey were connected the way she and Luke were connected. Twins not of the womb but of the Force. And she knew if there was any way she could save Ben, it would be through what she had taught Rey.

With all the energy she had left, she reached out with her love, told her son goodbye, and invited him home.

CHAPTER 17

REY LEAPT TO HER FEET, picked up Kylo Ren's lightsaber, and moved in for the kill.

Ren had stumbled backward onto the deck. Why he had done so, she didn't know—or care. All she wanted to do was end Kylo Ren's pitiful life right then and there.

Rey ignited his saber and rushed at Ren, impaling him with the blade.

He grasped his chest and cried out. And as she withdrew her saber, she heard what he must have heard that made him stumble. An echo in the Force.

Ben.

It was Leia's voice. Warm, kind, compassionate. A parent's love. And as the voice faded, Rey realized that it had faded for good.

Leia Organa had passed away. And Rey had just killed her son in a bout of rage.

Rey stood on the wreckage of the Death Star, splashed by the cold sea, feeling emptier than she had ever felt. How could she have let her temper take hold of her, once again? Kylo Ren might have been a great evil, but one did not match evil with evil. In her anger, Rey had disregarded all her teacher had taught, and now her teacher was gone. There would be no more lessons to learn. This had been the final lesson, and she had failed. She would never be a Jedi.

Rey extinguished the lightsaber and dropped it. At her feet, Kylo Ren groaned in pain, shifting an arm over the saber wound in his chest. Death hadn't taken him. Not yet.

Rey bent down to him. She blinked away tears. "Your mother," she said.

Ren regarded her with indifference, like a dying animal that knew its time was up. "Do it. Quickly." He closed his eyes, as if expecting to be finished off.

But there might be something else she could do. If he let her do it.

Rey propped Ren against a pylon. Then she placed her hand on his chest and sank into the Force, concentrating on her breath. His eyes opened again, in surprise. She met his gaze and held it. His eyes were windows into a damaged mind and soul, neither of which she could fix. But the wound in his chest, and even the scar on his face—those the Force could heal.

As she had with the vexis, she gave him some of herself.

After she was done, she sat back and caught her breath. Ren lay before her, still in shock at what had happened. His face showed no sign of the scar she had given him with her blade a year before.

She stood, light-headed and weak. "You're right, I did want to take your hand," she said, responding to what he'd said to her on Pasaana. "*Ben's* hand."

She left him lying on the wrecked Death Star catwalk, with waves crashing around him. After she had retrieved her lightsaber, she glanced back.

The fog had erased him from her sight.

The *Millennium Falcon* made the journey to Ajan Kloss without a hitch. The thrusters burned at the correct intervals. The landing gear deployed properly. Even the compressor made accurate adjustments to the engine pressure. It appeared that Jannah and her company had helped put the *Falcon* back in working order, and for that Poe was grateful. But having a fixed *Falcon* made little difference to their mission without the most important member of their team.

Rey had left them.

Poe landed the *Falcon* in the jungle clearing outside the cave, angry at himself. He had been the one who had begged that Rey be put on these missions, yet General Organa in her wisdom had continually told him that the girl wasn't ready. Now he had to tell the general not only had they failed in their mission, but they had lost Rey along the way. Finn had last seen her flying off Kef Bir in Kylo Ren's TIE fighter, having informed no one of where she was going or if she had found the Emperor's wayfinder. Perhaps she didn't want to put the rest of the team in danger, but they had already signed up for that by joining the Resistance. Rey's nobility masked an impulsiveness that might doom them all—and as the highest-ranking member of the team, Poe felt responsible for not curbing it. He had flunked the leadership test yet again.

But maybe there was something the general could do. During the battles of D'Qar and Crait, she and Rey had shared beacons. Maybe there was a way she could reach out to Rey or Rey could reach out to her. General Organa always had a backup plan.

Poe ran down the *Falcon*'s ramp, with Finn, Chewie, and the droids right behind him. Commander D'Acy met them at the entrance of the cave. "Poe! Something's happened."

There was very little activity in the cave, and those who were on duty hung their heads low. When Poe moved past her for a view of the command center, D'Acy addressed the others. "Finn—"

Finn also stepped forward with Poe. "This can't wait."

Spotting only a few officers at the consoles, Poe looked around the blockade runner. "We gotta see the general."

D'Acy let out a small breath. "She's gone."

Poe turned back to D'Acy. She said nothing else. He stood there, unable to move. All he could feel was the blaster wound on his arm, throbbing.

Chewbacca fell to the ground, shaking. When Finn leaned down to give him a hand, he swatted it away.

It had often been said that there was nothing more bloodcurdling than a Wookiee roar. It could also be said that there was nothing more heartrending than a Wookiee wail.

Kylo Ren stood at the edge of a beam, holding the hilt of his lightsaber and staring up at the sky. The waves in the surrounding ocean had subsided, but his confusion—his anger—had not. His mother was dead. He should be dead. The scavenger girl had defeated him, impaled him with his own blade. Yet she couldn't leave him to die. Just as his mother couldn't leave him without saying goodbye and sending him her love. Why was it that no one could ever leave him alone?

Storm clouds moved past to reveal the disk of Endor's forest moon. Darth Vader's ashes lay on that moon, and it was from there that his mask and helmet had been retrieved. For years Ren had meditated over those relics in the hope of communing with his grandfather, just as the voices in his head had communed with him.

But whenever Ren called to his grandfather, there was never a response. The silence taught him a lesson. Hope was a false prophet; it only led to crushing disappointment. For the past was past and the dead were dead, and nothing could bring them back. It was why Palpatine went to such lengths to stay alive. Because after this, there was nothing.

Or at least that was what Ren had thought, until his mother and Rey had brought him back from certain death and showed him the strength of resisting one's inner darkness.

He felt a presence behind him. And heard a voice. "Hey, kid."

Ren turned. It was Han Solo, dressed in the same clothes he had been wearing when Ren had killed him.

"I miss you," Han said.

Ren frowned. "Your son is dead."

"No," Han said. "Kylo Ren is dead. My son is alive."

Ren squinted at Han. "You're just a memory."

"Your memory," Han said. "It's not too late. Come home."

Home. Ren almost laughed at the suggestion. After all he'd done? There was no home for him. No one he could reconcile or reunite with. The last person who had loved him was dead. "It's too late. She's gone."

"Your mother's gone," Han said. "But what she stood for, what she fought for, that's not gone."

Ren turned away, telling himself this was nothing but a manifestation of his own guilt, trying to make him do something that was beyond his power.

"Ben."

Ren had often recoiled from his birth name, yet coming from Han this time it sounded different, as if it had been unmuffled and given breath. He was reminded of happier times, of the person he was, of the son who had been everything to his parents.

He regretted having repressed his birth name for so long. He had been so occupied with forcing Rey to accept her name that he hadn't realized he was the one who needed to accept his.

He doubted he could live up to that name now. "I know what I have to do," he said to Han, "but I don't have the strength to do it."

"You do."

The voices Ren had heard in his head had always told him how weak he was, how he couldn't survive unless he listened to them. Yet this voice said the opposite. It affirmed not what he couldn't do but what he could.

A strange feeling came over him. A tenderness. "Dad—"

"I know," his father said.

For some moments they looked at each other, father and son, Han and Ben. And in his father's eyes, Ben saw a pride and a joy he had always sought but never received from reaching out to his grandfather.

He was determined not to let his parents down this time. So he did what Rey had done. He made a choice.

Ben Solo took his lightsaber, the lightsaber he had plunged into his father's heart, and threw it as far as he could, so that when it fell it plunged into the heart of the sea, never to kill again.

CHAPTER 18

POE WAS NUMB.

The ointment Beaumont Kin had applied to his arm relieved the pain, but the numbness came from something deeper than a blaster wound. Something incurable. General Organa had been the guiding light of the Resistance since it began. Now they were all in the dark. Without her, they would never be able to win the fight against the First Order, let alone survive. The speech he had made on Crait about sparks and fires seemed like the words of a fool.

He leaned against a gurney in the base's infirmary. Stacked crates formed walls to offer patients a slim degree of privacy. "We came so close," he said to Kin. "I'm sorry."

Kin stayed silent as he wrapped a new bandage around Poe's arm. Commander D'Acy walked into the opening between crates. She looked as grim as when she had reported the news of the general's passing. "You need to see this," she said.

Kin and Poe followed her to the command center. "Kijimi's been destroyed," she said matter-of-factly, as if such terrible things were now commonplace—which they were. "A blast from a Star Destroyer."

"Impossible. It would take—" Poe hesitated. Zorii was on Kijimi. "No. No. No way a Star Destroyer—"

"It was from the new Sith fleet," D'Acy explained. "Out of the Unknowns."

At a communications console, Commander Rose Tico called up a holographic transmission that was broadcast galaxy-wide. It showed a dark gray Star Destroyer hovering over the brown orb of Kijimi. A superlaser on the Destroyer's underbelly fired a sustained blast at the planet. Kijimi appeared to pulse, as if absorbing the blast, and then the world collapsed on itself before exploding into fragments.

Poe felt part of his heart do the same.

Kin studied the hologram of the Star Destroyer. "The Sith sent the ship from Exegol. Does that mean all the ships in his fleet—"

"Have planet-killing weapons?" Poe said. "Of course they do. Every one. This is how he finishes it."

That was the bitter truth. Any planets and people who rebelled or refused allegiance would be obliterated. No one was safe.

"There's also a message," Rose said. "Listen. It's on every frequency." She amplified the volume. A voice spoke in a cryptic language Poe didn't know.

Kin translated the message. "'The Resistance is dead. The Sith flame will burn. All worlds surrender or die. The Final Order begins.'"

When Kin finished his translation, Poe noticed all eyes in the command center were on him. It was as if they expected him to have a solution to this.

"Leia made you acting general," Rose said. "What now?"

The holorecording ran on repeat, and Poe stood there, not knowing what to say, as Kijimi imploded, then exploded again.

C-3PO walked around the cave that Poe and Finn called Resistance headquarters. It wasn't much of a headquarters, in his data-driven estimation. A headquarters was, according to his preloaded language sets, a bustling industrial complex where thousands of workers went about their duties at peak efficiency to manufacture a valuable product, such as a droid. In this humid cave—which caused condensation to gather in his joints—there were only a hundred or so workers, and whatever labors they were assigned, none seemed to be efficient about them. Their shoulders drooped and their faces were inexpressive, which in C-3PO's calculations described the organic emotion of sadness.

An R2-series astromech droid wheeled toward him, beeping a warm welcome and showing none of the collective somberness. C-3PO responded in kind. "Hello, I'm See-Threepio, human-cyborg relations. And you are?"

The droid rolled back, swiveled his silver dome, and sniped. C-3PO was insulted. "My memory 'backup'? Why would a stubby astromech droid have my memory stored?"

The droid identified himself as R2-D2—as if that meant anything—and beeped that since they were best friends, he had stored an emergency backup of C-3PO's memory.

C-3PO huffed at such a ridiculous association. "Well, I'm quite certain I'd remember if I had a best friend."

To end the conversation, C-3PO headed toward the large blockade runner parked in the center of the cave. But the pesky droid whirred after him, extracting his data transfer arm. "You stay away from me with that!"

R2-D2 beeped that he'd never do anything to hurt C-3PO, even if the protocol droid no longer considered him a friend. The two had a long-standing history of working together.

Searching his memories, C-3PO found no instances of working with a unit known as R2-D2, or any astromech for that matter. But this R2-D2 was insistent they had.

"Whatever are you referring to? What history together?"

R2-D2 continued to babble in binary about Death Stars, Clone Wars, Luke Skywalkers, and Obi-Wan Kenobis, and the first time they met in a hovel on Tatooine. Then there were the years they'd spent together on Alderaan, serving Captain Antilles and Princess Leia, even traveling on the cruiser in this cave, the *Tantive IV*.

C-3PO scanned the blockade runner with his photoreceptors. Its crest did match that of the royal house of Alderaan in his database. Still, his memory had no record of royal service. "On a ship like that? With a princess? You're malfunctioning!"

C-3PO turned from the droid. Before he could take another step, all servomotor operations halted. His last independent computation was that the R2 unit had committed the droid equivalent of backstabbing by plugging his data transfer arm into C-3PO's rear-plate socket.

Finn sat in the area Rey had carved out for herself in the cave. What she had done on Kef Bir had upset him. It wasn't her throwing him back that hurt—he'd shaken that off soon afterward. It was that she had seemed to be on the brink of doing something that wasn't at all like her. The Rey he knew wasn't a killer. Yet when she had spun toward him, that's what he had seen in her eyes.

Ochi's droid rolled around on the ground, inspecting Rey's things. He pecked a training remote recharging at a generator, then zoomed away when it tried to zap him. Rey's books received some scrutiny, but he seemed leery of the dehumidifying field. Nonetheless, the droid took great interest in the various tools and components scattered on her workbench. The accordion tubing of his neck lifted so the cone of his head was on the same level as the bench top.

Finn snapped out of his funk when the droid started poking at the parts of the lightsaber Rey had intended to build. "Hey, don't touch that—that's my friend's."

The droid spun backward. "So sor-sorry. She is gone?"

"Gone," Finn said. "I don't know where."

The droid craned his cone toward Finn. "I miss her."

"Yeah, I miss her, too," Finn said. But thinking about her was only going to make him more miserable. He needed to get his mind off her. "So what's your name?"

The droid identified himself as D-O, but it was what the little chatterbox said next that had Finn running to find Poe.

The general's quarters were dark. She lay in repose on the bunk where she had passed. A sheet covered her, and under it her arms were crossed over her chest. After a lifetime of war, she appeared to be finally at peace.

Poe was not.

He knelt near her, hands clasped, at war with himself. Just a year earlier, he'd had no trouble imagining himself as leader of the Resistance. He had been so cocky and sure of his own abilities that he'd even tried to take command from Vice Admiral Holdo when he hadn't agreed with her decisions. But Holdo and General Organa had shown him how wrong he was. And instead of court-martialing him, General Organa had excused his disloyalty as youthful overconfidence and offered him a second chance in the Resistance.

He hadn't deserved it then—and he didn't deserve the command he was given now. He didn't have the experience or the wisdom of someone like the general. He was just a pilot with a big mouth. How could he lead anyone against a fleet of mobile Death Stars?

"I've got to tell you," he whispered to the general, "I don't know how to do this. I don't know what you saw in me. I'm not ready."

"Neither were we," someone said.

Poe had thought he was alone. In the corner, almost invisible in the shadows, sat their helper from Pasaana, General Lando Calrissian.

"Luke, Han, Leia—me." Lando walked over to Poe using a steel-tipped cane. "Who's ever ready?"

Poe stood and turned to Lando. "How did you do it? How do you beat an empire with almost nothing?"

Lando looked down at Leia. Several silent moments passed, and it seemed as if he didn't have an answer. But then he spoke with quiet certainty.

"We had each other. That's how we won."

This was said by the man who had once betrayed his friend Han Solo to save his city from an empire of another age. Yet Lando had made up for that betrayal by helping Leia rescue Han—and Han, in turn, had forgiven him.

General Organa had done the same for Poe. She had respected him not just as a pilot but as a friend. And friends didn't give up on each other after being wronged. They gave each other second chances.

Poe was not going to waste his second chance. He would live by General Organa's example and not fear that he had to lead the Resistance all by himself. For true leadership depended on the support and involvement of one's friends.

With Lando beside him, Poe paid his final respects to the woman who had never betrayed him.

CHAPTER 19

REY WATCHED KYLO Ren's TIE fighter burn.

She hadn't crashed it, nor had it malfunctioned on her trip to Ahch-To. Rather, she had landed the TIE on the mountainous island where she had trained, then set a torch to its engines herself.

During the journey, she had thought about many things. She thought about what Ren had said about her origin. She thought about her failures on the path to become a Jedi. She thought about her anger and her rage. She thought about Finn, who had been trying to help her when she tossed him back as if he had meant nothing to her.

She thought about Leia.

The worst feeling was knowing she could never go back to her teacher. She couldn't apologize. She couldn't endure Leia's disappointment. She couldn't ask for forgiveness. Because Leia had passed. And though she reached out to her teacher through the Force, as Leia had instructed her to do, the only voice Rey heard was her own.

She was alone. Truly alone.

It had been Rey's own inner voice that had compelled

her to go to Ahch-To. On the gloomy island of the ancient Jedi, she would follow Master Skywalker's example and spend the rest of her life as he had, in exile. And the galaxy would be safe from her abusing her power.

Rey picked up blackened wood from the sacred tree that had burned down since her last visit. She then walked closer to the fire, donning the hood of her capelet to protect her face from the heat. One by one she threw the pieces of wood into the fire, fueling it to consume the TIE fighter. When she was out of logs, she took out her lightsaber, the one Leia had given her, Luke's old blue blade. The hilt fit her hand well despite being made for another. She owed the weapon so much. On multiple occasions it had saved her life.

She threw it toward the blaze.

Before the fire took it, a human hand emerged from the flame to grab the lightsaber from the air. The hand belonged to a man Rey had believed dead. "A Jedi's weapon deserves more respect," he said.

"Master Skywalker," she said, stepping back.

He walked out of the flames. "What are you doing?"

Rey peered at him—*through* him. She hadn't reached out to him, but there he was, partly transparent yet present in the Force. He appeared both younger and somehow older than before, but his expression was more playful, almost childlike, with the hint of a smile. He wore his traditional Jedi robes and seemed less like a wild hermit and more like a monk at peace. Then again, she might just be seeing things, which was entirely possible given her visions.

Some of the island's avian porgs waddled up on rocks. Did they also see him? The closest one to her squawked, not telling her anything.

Luke gestured for Rey to sit down on a rock. She did. When she was ready, she explained herself. "I saw myself on the dark throne," she said. "I won't let it happen. I'm never leaving this place because I can't control my power."

She recalled the vision she'd had under Luke's tutelage, in which she'd seen the sea cave. Luke had told her to resist it, yet she had not. She had allowed herself to swim in its darkness and almost drowned.

"You saw the darkness in me when you trained me. You were right not to want to teach me more. I'm a threat to the galaxy, not a protector," she said. "That's why I've come here. I'm doing what you did."

He looked down at her and shrugged. "I was wrong."

She stared at him. Had the great Luke Skywalker, who had been so set in his convictions when she had last visited him, admitted an error?

"Even Jedi make mistakes," he said. "It was fear that kept me here."

His confession stunned her. The Luke Skywalker she had met had made grand accusations about the corruption in the Jedi Order. Yet now he seemed to accept that no one was perfect, including him.

She was definitely not perfect herself. "I did everything I was trained not to," she said. "I've drawn my saber first, attacked Ren, blind with anger."

Luke was not cross with her. In fact, he sounded like he understood. "Anger comes from fear. What are you most afraid of?"

Her answer came without thinking. "Myself."

"Because you are a Palpatine?" he said.

"You know?"

He nodded. "Leia knew it, too."

Was that why Leia had been so hesitant to send Rey out on missions? "She didn't tell me," Rey said. "Yet she still trained me."

Luke pulled up his robes so he could sit down next to her. "Because she saw your spirit, your heart. Like I do."

She shook her head. It was as if he couldn't see her—the true Rey—as he had seen her in the past. "The darkness is stronger in me than you know."

He leaned close to her. His hair, though ghostly, fluttered in the wind. "Rey, some things are stronger than blood. Confronting fear is the destiny of a Jedi. Your destiny. If you don't face Palpatine, it will mean the end of the Jedi. And the war will be lost."

He rose and his robes fell back to the ground. "Come with me. There's something my sister would want you to have."

Luke took her to his hut. It lay in a village of similar mound-like structures, built of stacked stones. He had told her before that the first Jedi had studied and meditated in these dwellings. The Caretakers on the island had maintained them for millennia.

Inside the hut's small room, Luke pointed to a brick in

the wall. Rey crouched, removed the stone, and found an object wrapped in burlap in the space behind. She took it out and unwrapped a lightsaber. The hilt was shorter and slimmer than Luke's, designed for a smaller grip.

Leia must have built this saber herself.

"It was the last night of her training," Luke said. "She told me she sensed the death of her son at the end of her Jedi path. She surrendered her saber to me and said that one day it would be picked up by someone who would finish her journey."

Holding her teacher's old saber, Rey blinked. Had Leia also had visions? Had she had a future vision of Rey?

"A thousand generations live in you now, Rey. But this is your fight. You'll take both sabers to Exegol. Just be wary. The evil in that place will weaken you. He will tempt you, deceive you, use your pain against you. But you must go."

Rey stood and turned around. "I can't."

Luke lifted a bushy eyebrow. "You can't?"

"I can't get there," she said. "I don't have the wayfinder. I destroyed Ren's ship."

"Rey," he said, "you have everything you need."

She considered the saber, then looked up. Master Skywalker was gone, with no sign of him, real or spectral, having ever been there.

She walked outside and returned to the site of the bonfire. A light rain had doused the flames and cooled what remained of Kylo Ren's TIE.

Something in the wreckage pulled at her.

Rey didn't move toward it immediately, as she had in the past. She looked at the TIE, the bent frame and charred cockpit. She could refuse the urge and walk away, and proceed to do as she had originally planned. But she also knew that whatever was in that wreckage would tug at her until she found out what it was.

Rey pushed aside some debris and reached into what had been the cockpit. Her hand danced along still-hot metal until it came to rest on something cold. She took it out.

It was a black pyramid in a resin frame, its form resembling the object she had found on the Death Star. A Sith wayfinder.

"Two were made," she said, echoing Ren's words on Kef Bir.

If the wayfinder on the Death Star had belonged to her grandfather, then this one must have belonged to his servant, Kylo Ren's grandfather Darth Vader.

Rey had traveled all the way to Ahch-To in the TIE and hadn't even realized it was in the cockpit with her. Had it hidden itself from her until now?

Regardless, the wayfinder was useless to her, even if it had the coordinates to Exegol. She had purposely incinerated her only transport off-planet and also any equipment to communicate with the rest of the galaxy. Her exile was assured.

She contemplated throwing the wayfinder off the cliff, squashing all future thoughts of leaving the island, when the sea began to rumble.

Porgs flew from their cliffside nest. Atop a neighboring hill shimmered the form of Master Skywalker. His eyes were closed and his arm was stretched out toward the sea.

From those waters rose an old X-wing starfighter—the fighter Luke had flown during the Battle of Yavin when he'd shot the proton torpedo to destroy the Death Star. It was the same one he had submerged in the sea to prevent him from ever leaving Ahch-To.

Luke had closed himself off to the Force during his exile, which would have made a feat like this impossible. But he was part of the Force now, and he lifted the X-wing onto the island without the need for pulleys or cranes, only his will.

He laid the fighter on the ground before her. Water flowed down its sides and leaked out of the cracks. Seaweed clung to the thrusters and the hull had rusted in many spots, but the cockpit remained sealed. And Rey knew the engines likely were fine, since they were part of their own closed system. The T-65 X-wings were hardy craft, built to last. A bath in ocean water was nothing compared with the infernos of space battles they had to withstand.

Rey glanced up the hill to offer a grateful nod. But of course Master Skywalker was gone again.

When C-3PO's systems came back online, an unspecified amount of time had passed, since his internal chrono had been reset. For some reason he stood in the middle of the cave on Ajan Kloss that was the Resistance's temporary headquarters. How had he gotten all the way over there? His last recollection was being in the base's droid maintenance section, hooked up to his counterpart. R2-D2 was set to download a backup of his memory before he went on an important mission.

The download must have been completed, because R2-D2 was next to him, withdrawing his data transfer arm. His logic processor calculated that there was a 93.8 percent chance that the download had temporarily restricted other functions, such as his memory storage routines.

"Ah! For a moment I didn't know who I was," C-3PO said. "Must have been a sensory glitch!" He faced his counterpart. "Artoo, have you heard? I'm going with Rey on her very first mission!"

R2-D2's response caused C-3PO's logic processor to return an error. "I . . . what? What do you mean I already have?"

But the astromech droid trilled that he had just received an important message and didn't have time to explain. C-3PO followed him toward the command center, where General Organa was conspicuously absent.

In the command center, Finn studied the hologram of a cloud-covered world and the data that swam around it. "This is everything you ever want to know for an air strike on Exegol."

Poe and Rose pored over the same data. "Except how to get there."

Providing all this information was D-O. The droid was plugged into the console and cheered on by BB-8 to keep sharing more. In Rey's workshop, D-O had revealed to Finn that he had a trove of information about the secret world of Exegol because his cruel master, Ochi of Bestoon, had intended to go there. The Emperor had supposedly ordered Ochi to capture a little girl from Jakku and take her to him on Exegol.

Finn and Poe reached the same conclusion that the little girl had to be Rey. For some nefarious purpose, Palpatine had wanted her alive.

Poe scrolled through holographic numbers around the clouds. "You see these atmos readings?"

Finn nodded. But it wasn't just the atmosphere that was concerning; it was the entire sector of space around the planet. "It's a mess out there. Magnetic cross fields—"

"Gravity wells, solar winds," Rose said.

"How can their fleet even take off in that?" Poe mused.

It was a valid point. Star Destroyers might be some of the toughest warships out there, but they weren't invincible. The conditions on and around Exegol could do irreparable harm to any kind of starcraft, particularly untested ships coming out of factories.

"I'm terribly sorry, but he insists!" C-3PO hustled into the command center, followed by a loud and lively R2-D2. "I'm afraid Artoo's memory bank must be crossed with his logic receptors. He says he's getting a transmission on a Resistance frequency—from Master Luke!"

R2-D2 whistled a tune of his own composition as he inserted his data arm into a console. A star map shimmered to life, with the symbol of an X-wing fighter speeding through space.

Poe tapped buttons on the console. "It's an old craft ID." His voice rose in surprise. "That's Luke Skywalker's X-wing."

"It's transmitting course-marker signals—on its way to the Unknown Regions," C-3PO said.

Finn peered at the X-wing and knew who piloted it. "It's Rey. She's going to Exegol." He traced her trajectory line in the star map. "She's showing us how to get there."

He looked over at Poe. What was decided next could determine the future of the Resistance—and the galaxy.

"Then we go together," Poe said.

Finn agreed. Rey could not do this all by herself. None of them could.

CHAPTER 20

POE ASSEMBLED his fellow officers, pilots, and soldiers around the blockade runner for a briefing on the mission that would make or break the Resistance. He let Finn and Rose Tico introduce the mission while allowing for an open discussion. Poe wanted to show that all of them would be involved in leading the Resistance.

"As long as those Star Destroyers are on Exegol, we can hit them," Finn said. A holoprojector had been erected on crates in front of the group, showing a spinning image of Exegol and the new First Order fleet.

"Hit them how?" asked Elna Zibsara, a rebel veteran who had flown in the Battle of Jakku.

"They can't activate their shields until they leave atmosphere," Rose said.

"Which isn't easy on Exegol," Poe added. "Ships that size need help taking off. Nav can't tell which way is up out there."

"So how do the ships take off?" asked Lieutenant Tyce, an ace pilot who was also Commander D'Acy's wife.

"They use a signal from a navigation tower, like this one." Poe pressed a button on his remote. The holo zoomed in on the planet, centering on a tall black tower with four vanes at the top.

"Except they won't," Finn explained. "Air team's gonna find the tower and the ground team's gonna blast it."

Lieutenant Vanik, a pilot whom Poe had recruited, reacted in surprise. "Ground team?"

Finn grinned. "I've got an idea about that."

D-O canted his head toward BB-8 and cooed. Poe, however, remained serious and stoic. "Once the tower's down, their fleet is stuck in atmo, with no shields, no way out."

"That's our chance," Lando said.

Snap Wexley wasn't buying it. "Shields or no shields, Star Destroyers aren't target practice. Not for single fighters."

"The Star Destroyers have a weak spot," Rose said. "Their axial cannons draw power directly from their reactors, which gives us a target. We think hitting the cannons might take out the main reactors and bring down the Destroyers."

Finn backed her up. "Fighters can take out their cannons if there are enough of us."

Nien Nunb, another hero of the Rebellion, whom General Organa had asked to helm the *Tantive IV*, protested in his native Sullustese.

"He's right, there's not enough of us," Lieutenant Connix said. "We'd be no more than bugs to them."

"That's where Lando and Chewie come in." Finn

gestured to the former gambler and the Wookiee. "They'll take the *Falcon* toward the Core. Send out a call for help to anyone who's listening."

Poe agreed. "We've got friends out there. They'll come if they know there's hope."

The assembled crowd grumbled and muttered in response. The Resistance had tried this before. General Organa herself had sent out a distress call on Crait. No one had come to their aid then. Why would they now?

"They will," Poe said forcefully. Much had changed since the defeat on Crait. The First Order had seized many more worlds in the galaxy and massacred entire populations to frighten others into submission. Their Star Destroyers menaced the skies not just of Endor and Kijimi, but of planets of peace and commerce like Bespin, Naboo, and even Coruscant. If the First Order's actions could rattle an ex-crewmate like Zorii Bliss—who never took a side and was hardly ever rattled—others would be rattled, too.

"The First Order wins by making us think we're alone. We're not. Good people will come to fight if we lead them. Leia never gave up and neither will we. We're going to show them we're not afraid. What our mothers and fathers fought for, we will not let die. Not today. Today we make our last stand for the galaxy." Poe paused to take in all their faces. "For Leia. For everyone we've lost."

Finn stood next to him. "They've taken enough of us. Now we take the war to them."

"May the Force be with us," Rose said.

"May the Force be with us," Poe repeated with everyone else. And in that rally cry, he felt what General Organa must have felt countless times—the joy of awakening the communal spirit. This was going to be the toughest challenge any of them had ever faced, and none of them had backed down. They were with him as they were with one another.

Finn hurried through the base as final preparations were made for launch. Support droids pulled the camouflage cover off the blockade runner's engines. The ground crew pumped fuel into starship tanks. The quartermaster handed out blaster rifles to the invasion force. Commander D'Acy gave Lieutenant Tyce a goodbye kiss at her A-wing. Finn gave Klaud a goodbye pat on his neck.

When Finn got to Poe's X-wing, C-3PO was there watching a crane load R2-D2 into the astromech socket. "I don't know any droids who would venture into the Unknown Regions," C-3PO said, gesticulating his arms. "But you're no ordinary droid."

R2-D2 beeped that indeed he wasn't.

Poe turned from the boarding ladder when he saw Finn. The two exchanged shoulder slaps and then a hug. But Poe didn't have his usual pre-battle swagger. He seemed distressed. "What's waiting for her out there?"

Finn shared Poe's concern. But whatever she was facing, they would be there for her.

"We'll see her again," he said to Poe. "I know we will."

Poe tapped C-3PO on the arm, causing the droid to look at him. But Poe said nothing else and heaved himself up the ladder into the cockpit.

Finn got out of the way of a loadlifter droid and went over to the transport lander *Fortitude*. Not only was he part of the invasion force, but Poe had made him a general. Recognizing his own inexperience as a strategist, Finn had recruited Jannah to help him lead the charge.

One of the soldiers boarding the lander surprised him.

"Rose?"

Rose Tico turned to him, holding an electro-shock prod in her hand. He went over to her, standing between her and the ramp. "You doing a checkup on the ship?"

"Volunteering," she said, tapping the blaster pistol holstered on her other hip.

"Oh, no, no, no." Finn didn't want her risking her life on a combat mission for which the chances of survival were slim to none. "Rose—"

"I'm going," she insisted. "You'll need an engineer."

"And a comms officer," said Lieutenant Connix, walking past them within earshot.

"And a history professor," said Beaumont Kin, right behind Connix.

The two boarded the lander. Finn sighed. Is this what being a leader was? Trying to tell your friends no and watching them go against your wishes anyway?

"Please move," Rose said to Finn. Her electro-shock prod hummed with energy.

He stepped back. "You going to stun me with that?"

Rose brought up the prod as if she were, then pulled back. "I only do that to deserters."

She smiled, and then so did he. On her necklace hung the symbol of her homeworld, a half-crescent of Haysian smelt. Its match had been worn by Rose's sister, Paige, who had perished during the retreat from D'Qar.

Finn touched Rose's medallion.

Over the past year, their paths had diverged as General Organa had deployed Rose's talents to develop new technology and techniques to prevent hyperspace tracking. But wherever life took them, Finn would forever be in debt to Rose for saving him on Crait. She was the best the Resistance had to offer—and more than anything else, one of his closest friends.

He squeezed the medallion and then let it go, stepping aside. She moved toward the ramp. Before she went through the hatch, Finn spoke again. "You know, I *am* a deserter."

She glanced back at him. "You are a deserter," she said, "of the First Order." She gave him a mischievous grin. "Still . . ." She pressed the trigger on her prod and blue energy danced around its tip.

Finn chuckled and they boarded the *Fortitude* together.

CHAPTER 21

AGAINST A DARK starscape hung the world of Rey's nightmares.

Exegol.

As the X-wing dove into the clouds, its sensors picked up massive engine signatures. Those signatures soon materialized into Star Destroyers armored in dark gray hulls, with red striping along the prows. Hundreds of the Destroyers drifted in neat rows while more lifted from giant bay doors on the planet's surface to join them.

Rey held her breath at the size of the fleet. It was far greater in number than what Finn's spy report had projected.

Fortunately, Rey landed without incident at the coordinates provided by the wayfinder. But the sight of all those Star Destroyers unnerved her. If they launched out of the Unknown Regions, no army or navy in the galaxy would be able to match the military might of the First Order.

Rey confirmed the details of her journey had been transmitted to the Resistance, then doffed Luke's old helmet, popped the canopy, and climbed out of the X-wing.

She stood on a darkling plain, staring up at a forbidding

citadel that floated above the ground. Lightning flashed around her. A chill wind made her shiver. Everything was cast in a blue-gray haze except the fortress looming before her. Its walls were as black as night. She saw no gate, yet she sensed a presence inviting her inside.

She knew she might never walk out if she entered it. She knew she might be consigning herself to pain and anguish and probably death.

Still she went.

Rey walked under the citadel and felt its immense weight above her, as if the pull of gravity had been partially reversed. Although no one else was there, her hand rested on the lightsaber on her belt, ready to draw.

The symbol of Ochi's dagger had been carved into the ground under the citadel. She came up to the dagger symbol and stepped lightly on the hilt. The ground beneath her started to move.

Rey found herself on the circular platform of a lift, lowering into the darkness. She sunk past hideous statues of what could only be the ancient Sith, their eyes sculpted in glares of evil. Sparks coursed around their forms. She refused to meet their stony gazes.

The lift landed in a grand hall. She walked off the platform and passed more of the giant Sith statues. She came upon what appeared to be a laboratory of sorts, with bubbling vats and tubes that dangled from the ceiling. She wasted nothing but a glance at the equipment. She had no desire to find out what terrible experiments had been performed there.

Energy flashed between a cleft in the rock wall, as if beckoning her. She entered the cleft and heard an eerie crooning from within. The sound increased in volume as she moved down the narrow corridor.

The corridor took her to a dais. She rounded it to see a black throne nestled between giant stone claws. It was the same throne she had seen in her vision, the one she knew to be the throne of the Sith.

No one sat on it.

The crooning became louder and she turned.

Thousands of cloaked and hooded beings filled the stands of a vast amphitheater that circled the chamber. A chasm billowing with energy separated them from her and the throne. The spectators chanted in a language she didn't understand.

"Long have I waited," someone whispered, close to her, "for my grandchild to come home."

She pivoted to see a mechanical arm descend from the darkness. Cables drooped along the armature's length, and at its end a gaunt ghoul of a man was pinned into a harness that resembled a metal claw. The man was repulsive to behold, yet Rey couldn't look away. Flashes of energy from the chasm revealed that his body was bent in the harness, hunched from a twisted spine. Under a thick hood, tumors bulged on his brow, and his face was a fold of wrinkles. His eyes were rheumy, with pupils of milky white. Tubes delivered fluids of some kind into his throat. What flesh clung to him had withered to the bone. And the black robes he wore couldn't hide his festering lesions and open sores. He was a man who was rotting alive—if alive he truly was.

He was her grandfather.

Poe had flown from one end of the galaxy to the other on hundreds of missions. He'd been tossed, shaken, jostled, and jerked, sometimes for hours at a stretch through treacherous tracts of space. But the journey through the Unknown Regions had so many twists and turns that even a veteran pilot like him felt on the verge of nausea.

He managed to keep it together, but he doubted many others in the Resistance fleet would. The important thing was that they lost no one on the way. The *Tantive IV*, the transport lander *Fortitude*, and all the starfighters made it through the strange red barrier and arrived at the coordinates Rey had transmitted. A planet enveloped in thick gray gloom rotated before them.

"Welcome to Exegol," Poe said over his X-wing's comm. The fighter squadron was under his command, and he'd put Finn in charge of the ground forces on the lander.

Poe plunged his fighter into Exegol's clouds. Rising toward the stratosphere was a gray-hulled Star Destroyer. Below it were scores more—scores upon scores, it appeared, according to his scopes.

"Great dark seas!" Aftab Ackbar exclaimed over the comm. He flew one of the Y-wings in their motley squadron. "Look at the size of that fleet!"

"No sign of the *Falcon* or allies," Tyce added from her A-wing.

"Just find that navigation tower," Poe said. "Help will be here by the time we take it down!" He said those words with the hope they would come true. The Resistance wouldn't last long against a fleet of this magnitude. They needed help.

The Resistance ships must have been detected, because the Star Destroyers started to unleash their cannons. A laser storm engulfed the sky, and the sheer torrent caught some starfighters, blowing them into chunks of white-hot metal.

"Stay at their altitude," Poe ordered. "They can't fire on us without hitting each other."

He showed the way, weaving through the blasts and diving toward the Destroyers. The others trailed him, descending to the same level as the massive ships.

Emergency alerts sounded. Enemy icons multiplied on Poe's tracking scopes. They might be out of reach of the Destroyers' cannons but not those of a new set of foes.

"Incoming TIEs!" shouted Snap Wexley, rolling his X-wing to the side.

Hordes of TIE fighters launched from what Poe assumed were underground hangars. These appeared to be a new variant, with triangular wings, red solar panels, and wing-mounted cannons and shield generators. They were also fast—faster than any other TIE Poe had encountered—and would overcome his squadron in mere moments.

Poe was about to call for evasive maneuvers when Finn brought some much-needed good news. "I see it!" he commed from the lander. "I've got a visual on the nav tower!"

Clouds drifted past, and Poe saw it, too—a giant industrial spire with four broadcast vanes. "Take my lead," Poe responded. "Lander, prep to unload the ground team at the base of the tower."

Poe jammed his flight yoke forward for a nosedive and activated his thrusters. It was all or nothing.

In the *Fortitude*'s cockpit, Finn stared at the navigation tower through quadnoculars. He searched for artillery, an energy shield, a troop garrison, or any defensive weaponry. All he spotted were steady blue-white lights on top of the tower.

Jannah came up to him from the troop compartment. "They ready back there?" Finn asked.

"Never been readier," she said.

Cockpit alarms halted her smile. Lieutenant Tyce's voice came over the ship's intercom. "The navigation tower—it's been deactivated! They're not transmitting from it anymore."

"What?" Finn returned the quadnocs to his eyes. The tower's lights had gone dark. But the fleet of Star Destroyers kept rising through the atmosphere, as if they were continuing to receive the navigation signal.

Snap Wexley joined the conversation. "The ships need that signal, so it's got to be coming from somewhere."

Finn put down his quadnocs. Through the viewport, he spied one Star Destroyer that didn't resemble the others. It was longer, larger, lacking the dark gray hull, and bristling with all sorts of weaponry.

Kylo Ren's flagship was there on Exegol. The *Steadfast*.

"Call off the ground invasion," Poe ordered over the comm.

"No," Finn said into his comlink. "The signal's coming from that command ship. That's our drop zone."

"How do you know?" Jannah asked.

Finn didn't know. And yet something inside him told him he was right. "A feeling," he said.

Tyce voiced her skepticism at Finn's notion of a drop zone. "You want to launch a ground invasion on a *Star Destroyer*?"

Finn rushed to the troop compartment, still speaking into his comlink. "I don't want to. But that ship's nav systems will have defenses against an air attack. If you give us cover to land, we can get to it—and take it out. We've got to keep that fleet here till help arrives."

"We hope," Rose said as she ran by him.

"We hope," Finn repeated.

Poe endorsed Finn's plan over the comm. "You heard the general. All wings, cover that lander!"

The lander's pilot shouted back to the troop compartment. "This'll be rough!"

Finn, Jannah, and the members of Company 77 from Kef Bir readied their rides. Rough was to be expected. The lander wasn't called *Fortitude* for nothing.

The troop lander eluded salvos of TIE laserfire on a fast descent, skidding across the *Steadfast*'s exterior in a shower of sparks. Before it had come to a complete stop, the hatch opened, the ramp extended, and out galloped shaggy orbacks ridden by ex-stormtroopers. Finn and Jannah led the pack, with BB-8 rolling beside them at his top speed.

"You're doing great, buddy! The tower's up ahead!" Finn said to the droid.

Not everyone in the invasion force was mounted. Connix, Rose, Beaumont Kin, and dozens of other soldiers ran out of the lander behind Jannah's company. They prepared to lay down suppressive fire against the enemy squads Finn fully expected to attack them.

Finn held the reins of his orbak. Unlike the frantic ride through Canto Bight on the fathier, this ride was invigorating. The orbak's hooves drummed a war beat against the hull. The bandolier of thermo-charges bounced against Finn's chest. The frigid wind, even on this polluted world, felt good against Finn's face. Though he'd only been able to practice riding for a short time on Ajan Kloss, he sat with confidence on his orbak.

"See this? After only one lesson!" he shouted to Jannah.

"You had a good teacher," Jannah said with a wink.

As they charged toward the aft of the Destroyer, the transmission tower came into view. But the conduit coils, generator boxes, turrets, and trenches presented tricky terrain for the orbaks to cross at full speed. Finn slid off his orbak and waited as Jannah and her company members also dismounted. They'd make it the rest of the way on foot.

Transports landed before them, impeding their path.

Out of the hatches jumped crimson-armored stormtroopers, a few equipped with jet packs. They immediately engaged the Resistance soldiers in a blaster fight. Finn, BB-8, Jannah, and her company were caught in the crossfire.

The bumpy superstructure had its benefits. Finn ducked behind a generator box and waved the others to follow him. They did, and the group hurried across the Destroyer, bobbing and darting around whatever they could use as cover.

While Jannah's company held off any attackers, Finn, Jannah, and BB-8 made a mad dash across the final stretch. Finn stopped before a hull panel near the base of the tower. "All right, Beebee-Ate, you're up!"

A squad of troopers rushed toward them. "I'll cover you!" Jannah yelled. She grabbed a thermo-charge from her bandolier and threw it. The squad was blown backward.

Finn fired his rifle at other troopers, giving the droid time to do his work. The droid extended his tool arm and unlocked the panel in the hull. Jannah, meanwhile, nocked an arrow in her bow and released. The arrow struck a jet trooper, propelling him back into a TIE fighter. The TIE careened and crashed into the Destroyer.

"Nice shot," Finn said. "Captain Grummart teach you archery?"

"Phasma," Jannah said, nocking another arrow.

Finn held back a chuckle. The former stormtrooper commander would have been irate knowing her training could be turned so effectively against her side.

BB-8 having done his job, Finn wrenched open the hull

panel. Jannah deposited both of their bandoliers in the hole, then set an activator and dropped it in. "This should do it."

When the panel slammed close, all three of them hurried away from it.

Despite the intense battle raging around him, Finn had the feeling of an even more consequential battle being waged somewhere down on Exegol.

Rey's grandfather hovered over the throne in his harness. Cast in the flickering light of the chasm, he looked more like a phantom than a living being. "I never wanted you dead. I wanted you here, Empress Palpatine," he said to her, gesturing to the dais. "You will take the throne. It is your birthright to rule here. It's in your blood. Our blood."

Rey stepped back from the throne, hand near the hilt of her lightsaber. "I haven't come to lead the Sith. I've come to end them."

"As a Jedi?" He sounded amused.

Rey steeled herself. "Yes."

"No," he said, drawing out the word. "I can feel your hatred. Your anger. Your thirst for revenge. You want to kill me. That is what I want. Kill me and my spirit will pass into you. As the Sith live in me, you will be Empress. We will be one."

Her grandfather had read her correctly. Rey *was* angry. She couldn't help it. But her anger was directed at one person—her grandfather. She was angry at what he had said.

Angry at all the evil he had done. Angry about being related to him.

And he could sense it.

"The time has come," he said, opening his arms to his audience. His acolytes cried out one shrill note in unison, then prostrated themselves. "With your hatred, you will take my life, and you will ascend as I did when I killed my master Darth Plagueis." He lifted a rotting hand toward Rey. "Now raise your saber and strike me down."

Rey was perplexed. Her own grandfather *wanted* her to kill him? Was this what Luke had been talking about, when he'd said she would be tempted and even deceived? She locked her feet in place, recalling her failures. She would fight her anger this time; she would not let it motivate her. "All you want is for me to hate. But I won't. Not even you."

He tilted his head toward her, but his cloudy eyes couldn't focus and he seemed to look beyond her. "Weak," he said. "Like your parents."

Though she knew little about her parents, the fact that they had hid her away from her grandfather spoke volumes about them. "My parents were strong. They saved me from you."

"Your master Luke Skywalker was saved by his father," he said. "The only family you have here is me."

The chamber rumbled. Dirt rained down as the ceiling split open, revealing a firefight in the sky. Lasers and explosions lit up the clouds. X-wings and other Resistance fighters engaged with the massive fleet of Star Destroyers and TIE fighters—and against such numbers, it was not a battle the Resistance would ever win.

"They don't have long," he said. "No one is coming to help them. And you are the one who led them here."

Rey didn't need him to provoke her guilt. She felt it already, watching an X-wing and then a pair of Y-wing bombers become fireballs.

"Strike me down," he continued. "Take the throne. Reign over the New Empire and the fleet will be yours. Only you have the power to save them all." As she stared at the battle, she felt the touch of the Force. It was so fast, so fleeting that she almost didn't recognize it.

"Refuse," her grandfather said, "and your new family dies."

More Resistance ships were shot down. There were so few of them, and so many TIEs and Star Destroyers. Her friends were all going to die, and there wouldn't be any Resistance left.

Her grandfather recognized how much those people up there meant to her. They were, as he said, her family. And she would do anything to save them.

She turned, forcing herself to nod. Though she said nothing, she knew her grandfather could feel her desperation. They were of the same blood, after all.

"Good." Her grandfather grinned, showing his rotted teeth.

CHAPTER 22

POE BLASTED TIE after TIE out of the sky. But the more he took out, the more that came back to take their place. There seemed to be an endless supply of the dagger-winged fighters, while the Resistance's own tiny squadron was dwindling in rapid fashion. The *Tantive IV* held back from the battle, but it wouldn't be long until the TIEs were able to swarm it.

There was a more urgent matter than the TIEs. The engine thrusters of the Star Destroyers had begun to glow. Normally, capital ships wouldn't fire their thrusters until they were in orbit, to prevent collateral damage to the planet and also minimize any atmospheric interference with the engines. But limiting harm to a planet was never a care of the First Order. Exegol was already a ruined world, so thruster burn couldn't harm it any further. And there were so many Star Destroyers in the fleet that losing even a couple in an engine accident wouldn't put a dent in it. Their priority was getting the warships into space and out of the Unknown Regions—which Poe's Resistance had to stop, at all costs to them.

"Those thrusters are hot," Poe told the squadron. "Finn, how we doing?"

"Give it one more sec—there it goes!" Finn said over the comm, and then Poe saw the navigation deck of the *Steadfast* explode.

"Nice one, Finn!" Poe switched channels to his starfighters. "Nav signal's down, but not for long." The Resistance had only minutes to spare until the Destroyers' flight engineers rerouted the signal to another transmitter. And Poe knew the First Order wouldn't fall for the same trick twice.

"Still no *Falcon* or backup," Snap reminded everyone on the channel.

R2-D2 made an inquiry on Poe's monitor. "I don't know, Artoo," he said to the droid. "Maybe they didn't find any allies. Maybe nobody's coming."

"What do we do, General?" Aftab Ackbar asked.

Poe dodged a TIE and reassessed the fleet. Unable to power their deflector shields in atmosphere, the Destroyers and their planet-destroying superlasers were all vulnerable. And since their minutes were counting down, the Resistance would probably never get another chance like this again.

He switched back to full broadcast. "We've gotta hit them ourselves."

Tyce scoffed openly on her comm. "What can we do against those things?"

"Whatever we can," Poe said. "Just stay alive!"

He wished he had something more inspiring to say, but

survival was their best option until reinforcements arrived—
if they ever did.

Finn skirted stormtrooper fire and ran with the others,
orbaks included, toward the lander. He was almost there
when he noticed a nearby turbolaser cannon wasn't firing at
the Resistance craft. He slowed to take a better look.

Jannah stopped and turned back. "Finn, let's go!"

Finn surveyed the deck, observing the same everywhere. "The surface cannons stopped," he said. "They're
resetting their systems."

"So?"

Remembering what Rose had said about the cannons,
Finn eyed the closest one. "I gotta do something."

"I'm staying with you," Jannah said.

Finn wanted to tell her that he could handle this alone.
But Rose had shown him on more than one occasion that
that wasn't what friends did. Her lesson had hit home,
because he'd been on the opposite end. How many times
had he gone to Rey and she'd pushed him away, believing
she could do things by herself?

Friends helped each other out. That was why they were
friends. And if the Resistance was anything at all, it was a
group of friends.

Finn nodded to Jannah and they headed to the cannon.
What looked small from the air was in reality an immense
double-barreled piece of artillery.

"This is the command ship," Jannah said. "We take it down, com-scan goes down."

"Affecting every Star Destroyer in the galaxy," Finn said. He was encouraged she was thinking along the same lines as him—they were both ex-stormtroopers, after all.

"This could throw the whole First Order fleet into chaos," she said.

They didn't even need to tell each other what to do. Finn started climbing the side of the cannon while Jannah drew an arrow from her quiver to provide cover. As of the moment, the jet troopers hadn't seen them branch off from the others.

But Rose had noticed. Her voice crackled over his wrist comm. "Finn! Where are you? Lander's leaving!"

"Go without us," he said into his comlink. "We're taking this whole ship down!"

"What? *How?*"

"You'll see from the lander," Finn said. "Rose, please. Go. Take care of yourself."

He heard BB-8 moan in the background before he muted his comlink. He couldn't argue with Rose. Not this time.

Crawling over the top of the cannon, he spotted the *Fortitude* launching from the Star Destroyer. Now it was just him and Jannah with the weight of a thousand worlds on their shoulders.

Ben Solo was strong in the Force, thanks to his mother. But he also had his father's luck, at least at the moment.

For it was by luck that he found a working TIE fighter in the Death Star ruins on Kef Bir. And it was by luck that the craft was a TIE scout with a hyperdrive. And it was by luck that Ben had managed to intercept Rey's course-signal markers so he could navigate a path through the Unknown Regions to Exegol.

Or maybe it wasn't luck. Maybe luck was just another name for the Force.

After landing his TIE next to the X-wing of his former Jedi master, Ben scrambled down a Sith statue into Palpatine's underground chambers. He hurried past the laboratory and hoped his luck would hold up long enough for him to join Rey. He had already reached out to her very faintly to say he'd come, but he had to hide his presence immediately afterward. If Palpatine knew he was there, Ben might never get to Rey in time or in one piece.

That still might not happen anyway.

Crimson-armored troopers fired at him as he ran toward the cleft in the rock wall. Drawing his pistol, Ben blasted them back. They were replaced by warriors of another breed, emerging from the cleft armored in makeshift metal and wielding rusty weapons.

Ben used to command the Knights of Ren, but he knew they wouldn't listen to any order he gave them now. Their true leader was Palpatine.

Ben fired at them, but it was useless. His blaster bolts bounced harmlessly off their armor. He dropped his pistol and clenched his fists. They closed in and attacked.

Perhaps the Solo family luck had finally run out.

"The ritual begins!" her grandfather proclaimed.

The throng behind Rey roared in approval as her grandfather addressed them. "She will draw her weapon. She will come to me. She will strike me down and take her revenge."

His words slithered into her mind. As terrible as it sounded, his proposition made sense. If she did what he said, if she struck him down with her blade, she could deliver a mortal blow to the First Order. She could call off the fleet, save her friends, and put a stop to the war for good.

Another presence reached out to her again. A vague plea in the Force. Was it Luke or Leia, trying to tell her to resist?

The armature lowed her grandfather toward her. "And with a stroke of her saber the Sith are reborn—and the Jedi are dead!"

She felt that presence again, not a light tap or touch, but a forceful tug. Followed by a cry for help.

It wasn't Luke or Leia. It was Ben. He was on Exegol, in the chamber outside the corridor. And he was being attacked, with nothing to defend himself.

"Do it," her grandfather said to her. "Make the sacrifice."

She unclipped Luke's lightsaber from her belt, kept it behind her back, and as her grandfather twitched in eager anticipation, she let go of it.

Ben was surrounded by the Knights of Ren: Vicrul, Ap'lek, Cardo, Trudgen, Ushar, and Kuruk. They had him bloodied and beaten. Weaponless. A blow away from complete submission.

It was a blow they would never land.

Ben reached behind his shoulder and grabbed the lightsaber Rey had sent him through their link in the Force. It was the lightsaber he had once wanted to destroy. The lightsaber of Luke and Anakin Skywalker.

He ignited it and reminded the Knights of Ren why he had been their leader. He went at them without anger or glee, but with all the focus of one trained as a Jedi. And one by one each of the Knights fell to his blade, Vicrul, Ap'lek, Cardo, Trudgen, Ushar, and Kuruk all skewered or slashed. He showed them mercy by giving them the quick deaths they had refused to give others.

After the battle was done, Ben ran through the cleft in the wall and joined Rey before the throne of the Sith.

She didn't say anything, but he felt her gratitude in the Force. She did not want to face her grandfather alone. He would not let her.

Ben lifted Luke's saber and Rey ignited another blue blade in her possession, which had to be his mother's. Leia's.

Leaning backward in his harness, Palpatine regarded them both with a sneer.

"So be it. Stand together, die together," the old man said.

He raised his hands and drew their very essence in the Force from them, then sent it back at them as raw, violent energy. Their lightsabers absorbed the first wave, but during the second and third Ben felt his grip on the hilt weaken as his life ebbed away. And the energy only seemed to gain in strength the longer Palpatine attacked.

Rey wavered, and so did Ben as the energy overcame their blades and bit into their physical bodies. Ben's flesh burned, but the real pain came from within—the energy ate at his soul.

Palpatine smiled as his own body began to be revived. "The life force of your bond, a dyad in the Force. A power like life itself, unseen for generations," he said.

Ben could no longer withstand the intense waves of energy flung at him. Neither could Rey. Both dropped their sabers and collapsed to the stone floor.

Palpatine laughed. "And now, the power of two restores the one true Emperor!" The Sith acolytes thundered their approval.

When the attack ended, Ben bolstered himself for one final charge.

CHAPTER 23

POE LAUNCHED his last set of proton torpedoes at a Star Destroyer superlaser. They struck their target dead center and the world-destroying weapon was neutralized.

"This is it!" Snap Wexley hollered over the squadron's channel. His torpedoes also found their mark on another Destroyer's superlaser, blowing it apart.

But there remained scores of Destroyers with their weapons intact. Poe could have had a dozen squadrons under his command and he still wouldn't have been able to dismantle them all. He also had another problem on his hands. The effort to torpedo the superlasers had taken the squadron's focus off the TIE fighters, which only grew in number. Entire squadrons chased down individual Resistance fighters, creating death traps Poe's pilots couldn't escape.

Kallie Lintra was the latest casualty. Eight TIEs came at her A-wing from all directions, firing their cannons. She took out three, and the TIEs shot down two of their own, but Kallie's A-wing was turned into a blazing wreck.

Poe took a deep breath. They'd lost her sister, Tallie,

when TIE missiles hit the hangar of the *Raddus* during the evacuation of D'Qar. Now they'd lost Kallie, too.

R2-D2 shrilled a warning that the three minutes had expired, which Snap Wexley confirmed. "Fleet's locking on to another navigation signal. They're gonna split!"

Lieutenant Vanik shouted over the comm. "Watch your starboard, Wexley!"

Poe sideslipped between two TIEs to find and help Snap, even though it sounded like the pilot had it handled. "Yeah, I see 'em—"

When Poe located Snap's X-wing on his scope, the ship's icon blipped, showing it doing a snap roll, but then the icon vanished.

"No!" Poe yelled. His cockpit canopy darkened to shield him from a bright explosion.

Snap had just made the ultimate sacrifice for the Resistance.

So, too, had Lieutenant Vanik, whose A-wing also disappeared from Poe's tracker. As had most of the other fighters in Poe's squadron.

Swooping around a Destroyer, Poe discovered he would soon add to their number. More than two dozen TIEs raced at him. He triggered his cannons, weeding out some, but that made little difference. One of them was going to get a lucky shot at him.

"Alpha Leader, do we retreat?" Tyce asked.

Poe hated the idea of retreating. But even in his final

moments, as leader of the Resistance, he was responsible for all of them. His life might end in the skies of Exegol, but he couldn't let the same fate befall the Resistance. A spark had to remain.

Before he could issue his last order for the Resistance, half the TIEs ahead of him scattered while the other half burst into flames. A smooth voice came over the comm. "I hear Leia needs pilots?"

Poe swung his X-wing around to find a massive armada descending through the atmosphere. There were ships of all makes and models—starfighters and tramp freighters, corvettes and capital ships. He saw a Ghtroc 720 and a VCX-100. A *Firespray*-class patrol craft flying with a *Pursuer*-class enforcer. Wookiee gunships and Gauntlet and Durosian fighters. Even a few old Z-95 Headhunters and a restored Cronian battlebird. These were but a few of the thousands of vessels arrayed before him.

Leading them all was one antiquated YT-1300 freighter, the *Millennium Falcon*.

Poe screamed with joy. "Look at this—*look at this*!"

For once, Aftab Ackbar didn't sound anxious. "The allies, they're here!"

"The whole galaxy's here!" Poe said. The gambler and the Wookiee had done it.

The *Millennium Falcon* sped past Poe's X-wing toward the Star Destroyers, its cannons firing away. The armada followed, pelting the Sith fleet with laserfire, concussion missiles, and proton torpedoes.

Numbers weren't a problem anymore. For the first time in the war against the First Order, the Resistance had the advantage. They had the ships.

They had the people.

The Star Destroyers buckled under the attack. They were so close together, many collided. Others lost their repulsors and began to tumble toward the surface. Gigantic vessels armed to destroy planets could not destroy the smaller vessels of the Resistance.

Poe left the Destroyers to the armada and concentrated on the TIE fighters. Reenergized by the appearance of the allies, he started chasing down TIEs, shooting them from the sky. A second X-wing joined him in the attack, not only replicating his tricky maneuvers but often blasting the pursued TIEs before he could.

Poe went wide with his question. "Who's that flier?"

"You know who, spice runner," the other pilot commed back. A wild "hey-heeeey!" echoed in the background.

Hearing their voices exhilarated Poe. "Zorii! You made it!" Somehow she had escaped Kijimi in time and was flying by his side with little Babu Frik in the cockpit. With the last-minute emergence of the fleet, Zorii among them, Poe felt something he hadn't felt in a long time.

Hope.

"The *Falcon!*"

Finn stood atop the cannon to watch the freighter

descend into the atmosphere. On the *Steadfast*'s hull below, Jannah gasped at the countless ships that arrived with the *Falcon*.

Finn shook his fist in the air. "I knew Lando would do it—I knew it!"

Red-armored jet troopers rocketed toward them, obscuring their view of the ships. While Jannah kept the troopers at bay with her arrows, Finn got back to work on the cannon, opening an access panel. He wasn't an engineer like Rose; he didn't know much about starship technology, but when it came to blasters and cannons, those had been in the First Order's curriculum.

Finn yanked a thick clutch of wires from the cannon. They sparked and the cannon rotated when he touched the wire ends together. "Okay, we're hot!" he said.

Holding the wires, he jumped back down to Jannah. The wires pulled farther out of the cannon but were long enough to reach the hull. He handed a bunch of them to Jannah and then touched two of his wires together. There were more sparks, but the cannon's turret swiveled down, its double barrels pointed at where the primary generator was housed on the *Steadfast*'s navigation deck.

"Never another kid," Finn said.

"Not even one," Jannah said. She tapped the ends of her wires against each other, causing a much bigger spark than Finn's.

In one booming blast, the cannon unloaded all its firepower into the *Steadfast*.

A crater opened in the Destroyer's hull, belching thick black smoke. But that was only the initial damage. If Finn's aim had been accurate, there should be more to come.

There was.

The *Steadfast* shook. Destruction of the power generator sent electrical surges throughout the ship. Fires erupted across the decks, followed by small explosions, then larger ones.

Yet again, working sanitation detail as a stormtrooper cadet had proved useful. That miserable experience showed him all the places, whether they be on Starkiller Base or Star Destroyers, where no one wanted to go. All the weak spots.

But the weakest spot in the First Order was the blind arrogance of its leaders. Finn could picture Allegiant General Pryde on the bridge, yelling at his officers, wondering what could have possibly gone wrong. Who could have done this?

FN-2187 and TZ-1719, that's who, Finn wanted to tell him.

The *Steadfast* began to fall from the sky. Finn took Jannah's hand. If there was a cause worthy of dying for, it was this—for his friends in the Resistance. For Lando and Leia, for Chewbacca and BB-8, for C-3PO and R2-D2, and of course for Rose, for Poe, and for Rey.

Rey had fallen next to Ben on the stone floor, drained beyond measure. She saw through the open ceiling that the sky battle had turned for the Resistance but knew it would be short-lived. Her grandfather was far from defeated.

He stood tall in his rejuvenated body, no longer restrained in the harness. Lifting his arms, he addressed the throng of Sith acolytes in the amphitheater. "Look at what you have made," he said to them.

Their chant boomed in the chamber. It was so loud Rey barely heard Ben groan and push himself to his feet. Rey tried to move, but her muscles wouldn't function. Her eyes wouldn't even open. Her grandfather's attack had taken almost everything from her. All she could do was listen.

What she heard only deepened her despair. "As once I fell," her grandfather snarled, "so falls the last Skywalker."

Through her connection to Ben, she felt the Force slam into him as her grandfather used the dark side to shove Ben toward the crevice. Ben's body smacked against the edge, shattering the rock and plummeting into the chasm. And then their connection broke.

In one swift move, her grandfather had killed Ben.

Now it was just Rey, lying before the throne. And if she didn't find a way to stop her grandfather, no one else would. The galaxy would be doomed.

"Do not fear their feeble attack, my faithful," he said to his disciples. "Now you will witness the power of the dark side! Nothing will stop the return of the Sith!"

Rey gathered the strength to open her eyes, just in time to see her grandfather lift his arms toward the ceiling. She had to squint when blue electricity spewed forth from the crevices in the floor to concentrate around her grandfather's hands. The energy then shot upward as a beam, through the open ceiling, and spread across the sky.

Poe's exhilaration turned to panic as a massive cyclone of energy erupted from the planet's surface. It engulfed his X-wing in a wave of electricity. Alarms rang out, his cockpit display blinked, and he fought to maintain altitude as his fighter went tumbling. "Artoo, all systems are failing!"

The astromech squealed in response. Poe hit the emergency comm. "Does anyone copy?"

No one did. All around Resistance-aligned ships were in the grip of the electrical storm. Illumination fizzled out across their bows. Engines failed. Many vessels lost power and crashed into each other. The Sith fleet, however, remained untouched.

Poe managed to right his X-wing, forgoing his display to rely on his own two eyes. But the larger capital ships required more advanced systems to stay aloft. The *Tantive IV* began to plummet toward the planet, and then one of its thrusters detonated.

Poe was powerless to stop the blockade runner from exploding.

CHAPTER 24 \\\

"BE WITH ME."

Rey lay on her back in the throne room, staring through the opening of the ceiling, saying those words. She watched the ships of the Resistance crash and burn. She wanted to help them but she didn't know how. All she could do was reach out as her teacher had told her to do, to call on those who had come before, and hope.

"Be with me," she said. "Be with me."

The battle vanished into night. A void of endless black. She stared into the darkness, searching for a light. She glimpsed one at the edge. Dim, but getting brighter. As was a light at the other edge. And then one in the middle. And then another, and another, until she was witnessing the birth of stars. And with each star, a voice.

These are your final steps, Rey. Rise and take them.

Bring back the balance, Rey, as I did.

Be the light. Find the light.

Alone, never have you been.

Every Jedi who ever lived lives in you.

The mind of a Jedi can move mountains. But the heart of the Jedi can move souls.

The Force surrounds you, Rey. Feel the Force flowing through you, Rey. Let it lift you. We stand by you, Rey.

Rey, the Force will be with you, always.

There were so many up there—so many stars, so many voices—Rey could not keep track. But there was a light inside her that shone brighter and spoke louder than all the others.

Stay here. I'll come back for you, sweetheart. I promise.

She looked deep into that light and saw there were two. A binary star. And though the voice that said those words was her own, the love behind them was not.

Rey pushed herself up to her knees and then to her feet. She stared at her grandfather, who had stolen some of her youth and Ben's for himself. Many of his wrinkles had disappeared. The cloudy film had cleared from his eyes to reveal small yellow pupils.

He might have rejuvenated himself, but to her he still looked like a sad old man.

He regarded her with irritation. "Let your death be the final word in the story of the Rebellion. You are nothing. A scavenger girl is no match for the power in me." He rose from the throne, pointing his hands at her. "I am all the Sith."

Rey summoned Leia's lightsaber to one hand, Luke's to the other. "And I am all the Jedi."

He blasted her with all his anger in the dark side. She

crossed the blades and held firm, feeling a thousand presences supporting her. Her blades did more than absorb her grandfather's energies. They deflected them back at him and the chamber around him.

Cracks opened in the walls. The amphitheater began to collapse. Sith acolytes scurried down tunnels. The spiked throne was caught in a stream of energy and exploded.

Struck by his own dark power, Palpatine shrieked as his flesh, muscle, and bone melted away, until nothing was left. Not even ash.

Rey fell to the floor as rubble rained down around her.

Poe breathed a sigh of relief. As suddenly as the electrical storm had struck, it had ended. It had taken a fair number of Resistance ships and pilots, but the majority of the fleet had made it through intact. And as long as they were alive, they could fight the First Order.

R2-D2 brought the X-wing's primary systems back online after the storm's effects had faded. Poe switched to the lander's channel. "Finn! You guys okay?"

Rose answered instead. "Finn didn't board the lander."

"What?"

"They're still on the command ship," she said.

Poe didn't ask anything more. He banked away from the TIEs and accelerated toward the *Steadfast*, which had started to tumble toward the surface. On its navigation deck, he spotted two figures amidst the flames—Finn and Jannah.

Poe gunned the engines toward them. But then the *Steadfast* went into free fall and Finn and Jannah slid across the deck. Poe soared overhead, unable to reach them.

"Alpha Leader, what are you doing?" Lieutenant Tyce barked over the emergency comm.

"I see them," Poe said. "I'll double back."

"You won't make it!" Tyce said.

"Trust me," he said, looping his X-wing around for another pass. "I'm fast!"

Lando intruded on the comm once again. "Not as fast as *this* ship. Hold on, Chewie!"

The *Millennium Falcon* tore through the flaming wreckage of the Star Destroyer. Beams screeched as they broke around it, but the *Falcon* stayed far enough ahead to avoid being struck. Poe, however, a few seconds behind, had to bank his X-wing to port or be crushed.

When he turned his X-wing around, the deck on which Finn and Jannah stood had split apart and was tumbling away with other pieces of the *Steadfast*. The deck must have also pulverized the *Falcon*, because there were only chunks of hot metal where Poe expected to see it.

Poe hadn't made it in time to save Finn and Jannah, and now they'd lost Chewie, Lando, and the *Millennium Falcon*. Why couldn't he have been the one instead?

"Chewie, you got the kids?" came Lando's voice over the comm.

One chunk of metal didn't drop like the rest. It rose. It was the *Millennium Falcon*. On top a Wookiee emerged from a hatch and two humans scrambled across the hull to him.

Poe exhaled—Finn, Jannah, Chewie, and Lando had survived. He soared high into the atmosphere to escape the world-shaking explosions. The battle had been won.

Finn dropped through the *Falcon*'s hatch. An old rebel pilot named Wedge Antilles, who had joined Lando and Chewie, helped him and Jannah down. Instead of rushing to the turrets as Wedge and Jannah did, Finn went to the first console he could find and initiated a sensor sweep for Luke Skywalker's X-wing.

While the scan progressed, Finn noticed a flurry of activity on Resistance channels. Reports were being received from all over the galaxy of star systems now in open rebellion against the First Order. Bespin, Jakku, Naboo, Corellia, Lothal, Thyferra, Coruscant.

The Resistance had done it. The spark that General Organa had lit had become a flame. The First Order would fall and a new age in the galaxy would begin.

But Finn couldn't rejoice in the victory. The *Falcon*'s sensors had finished one sweep of the surface and so far had not shown a sign of the X-wing.

Trusting his instincts, Finn did something he'd never done before. He closed his eyes and reached out to his closest of friends, hoping he could help her in some way if she needed it.

Rey.

Ben's luck held out. He managed to break his fall down the chasm by catching a protruding ledge. He then pushed all pain from his mind and clawed up the chasm back into the throne room.

Rey lay in a heap near the shattered throne.

Ben knelt down to her and picked her up in his arms. She was cold. She did not move. He felt nothing from her.

Her grandfather had taken her life.

Ben remembered what she had done on Kef Bir. She had given him some of her life so that he could live. This part of her was still inside of him.

Following her method, he placed his hand on her waist and sank into the Force. He found her spirit within him and gently returned that essence to her, along with what he had left of his own.

She woke slowly, stirring, her eyes opening to look up at him. At first she seemed startled, but that soon changed. She smiled, staring into his eyes, and reached up to kiss him.

"Ben," she said.

He smiled back at her—Rey, this scavenger girl who had salvaged his life—until the world around him faded away and he went home.

CHAPTER 25 ◣◣◣

ON THE FOREST MOON of Endor, an Ewok elder sat on a tree branch with a wokling. In the language of the ones from beyond, the elder's name was Wicket and the younger one was Pommet. But in their own language, they just called each other Father and Son.

The wokling could not take his eyes off the silver triangle in the sky. It had arrived days earlier and hovered like an arrowhead looking for a target. The wokling asked questions about it, many questions, but his father did not answer them. "You will have the rest of your life to hear stories of such things," his father had said. "Right now you must learn about this forest and this world where you live."

But the wokling didn't want to learn about this forest. He didn't want to learn about this world where he lived. He wanted to learn about the worlds beyond. He wanted to know why the silver triangle was in the sky. He wanted to know if it was an arrowhead from the Golden One.

For a long time the father looked at the vessel that the ones from beyond called a Star Destroyer. It reminded him of the great war and of the human princess who had come to their aid. Even after his people had tried to eat the princess's friends, the princess had pledged her tribe to help Wicket's tribe defeat the white-shelled barbarians and take the death moon out of the sky.

For years afterward there had been peace, and the Ewok tribes had flourished. But dread gripped the father when he first saw the silver triangle. Was it an omen that another death moon would soon darken their days?

As father and son looked up that morning, the silver triangle fell from the sky and disappeared. The father sighed in relief. "That, my son, is a blessed sign of the Golden One," he said.

He placed an arm around his child and held him tight.

"Thank the Maker! Thank the Maker!"

C-3PO pushed his brass-colored legs faster than their designer-recommended limit. Preservation routines informed him that the legs could break. His joint bolts were old. The servomotors had rusted in the humidity. And there were no replacement parts on Ajan Kloss for a Cybot Galactica unit of his vintage.

But there was another set of routines that held greater priority in his programming than preservation. And that was protocol.

Protocol demanded he get out of the Resistance base as quickly as he could to welcome those volunteers coming home. Protocol also demanded he check on his counterpart.

Outside the base, the few Resistance ships that had survived the Battle of Exegol landed in the jungle clearing. C-3PO's photoreceptors identified BB-8 rolling out of a transport lander with Commander Rose Tico. The ball droid whistled merrily when joined by a smaller tread-wheeled droid whose designation C-3PO had learned was D-O.

C-3PO saw Finn run out of the *Falcon* to greet Poe. The pilot's left arm was in a sling, but that didn't stop him from giving Finn a hug.

The Wookiee Chewbacca was also there, receiving Captain Solo's medal from Maz Kanata. Nearby, Professor Beaumont Kin and then Finn embraced Klaud, who blushed green with embarrassment, while Commander D'Acy did the same to Lieutenant Tyce, who did not blush.

Next to the transport, the riders from Jannah's company were teaching the Abednedo pilot C'ai Threnalli how to feed an orbak. C-3PO stayed well away from those wild beasts.

Noticeably absent from the homecoming was Rey. But the probability of her survival wasn't something he could determine with any degree of accuracy. Beings who had talents in the Force, like Master Luke and Princess Leia, seemed to defy all odds.

C-3PO caught Poe and Zorii exchanging meaningful looks across the clearing. Lieutenant Connix was laughing at some joke. Chewbacca wrapped Rose in his shaggy arms. Jannah sat on some crates, chatting with General Calrissian.

C-3PO's leg joints ground to a halt when he got to Poe's X-wing. The fighter had dents from bow to stern. Paint peeled off the hull where fire hadn't blackened it. The laser cannon tips were bent, and the nose cone looked like a bite had been taken out of it.

But his counterpart, standing near the X-wing's landing gear, seemed in very good condition for a droid who had come out of a war zone.

"Thank the Maker!" C-3PO exclaimed.

R2-D2 wobbled from side to side on his two legs and let out the happiest beeps C-3PO had ever heard. "Yes, Artoo, I'm fine, except for a stiff servo joint. And I'm glad to see you, too. We've won, you know—we've won!"

The intensity of seeing R2-D2, when C-3PO had determined there was zero probability of ever seeing him again, flipped some bits in his neural network. This caused a memory file that R2-D2 had restored to be accessed and read. It was a record of the moment when C-3PO's maker had fitted a photoreceptor into his eye socket and he had experienced the visual spectrum for the first time. The initial image his photoreceptors had captured was of a blue-and-white astromech.

The circuits that modulated his mood buzzed in jubilation. No wonder he and R2-D2 were strong counterparts—the two had been together since C-3PO's original power-on!

The sound of an engine familiar to C-3PO kept his mood circuits in that excited state. "Did you hear that?" he asked R2-D2. His torso servomotors tilted so he could look up into the sky.

An X-wing fighter—Luke Skywalker's X-wing, C-3PO's

analysis confirmed—touched down. The cockpit canopy opened, and Rey climbed out.

The girl from Jakku had made it. She had survived the battle and helped save them all. Princess Leia would have been so proud of what she had done. C-3PO had to tell Rey—tell her right away.

As C-3PO processed the command to move his legs, his counterpart did something that he could have never predicted. R2-D2 swiveled his dome and beeped a sentiment only organic beings expressed to each other.

C-3PO did not move toward Rey. He could tell her what the princess would have thought soon enough. Instead, he laid his metal hand on R2-D2's dome and kept it there.

Protocol demanded it.

EPILOGUE

ONCE THERE WAS BOY who was good of heart. Enslaved as a child, the boy lived with his mother and had a talent for building things out of spare parts. He also had another gift, one he couldn't explain. His mother said he had special powers. The man who freed him said he had the Force. The boy studied and trained, and as a young man became a Jedi Knight of great renown. His teachers speculated he might be a figure of prophesy, a chosen one to bring balance to the Force. But the choice he made was not one they had foreseen. He betrayed his teachers, murdered his friends, and fell under the sway of a master crueler than any he had known.

The boy was called Anakin, the young man Darth Vader. Only Anakin was Skywalker by name, but both were Skywalkers by blood.

Once there were twins, a boy and a girl. Separated at birth, the boy was raised as a moisture farmer, the girl a princess. Both had a gift they couldn't explain. War brought them together when they were older, during which the girl became a commander of rebels, the boy the last of the Jedi. The two also discovered that they were siblings and that

Darth Vader was their father. The boy redeemed his father from the darkness, while the girl righted her father's wrongs as a galactic leader for decades to come.

The twins were called Luke and Leia. Only Luke was Skywalker in name, but both were Skywalkers by blood.

Once there were twins, not of blood, but of the Force. This dyad was made up of a girl and a boy. The boy was raised by both parents in a loving home, the girl by herself in a desert scrapyard. Both had a gift they couldn't explain. War brought them together when they were older, during which the boy became the leader of a hostile military, while the girl became the symbol of resistance against him. Despite a consuming darkness, the girl returned the boy to the light.

The girl was called Rey, the boy Ben. Only Ben was a Skywalker by blood. Rey was a Skywalker by choice. She chose to take the family name of her teachers, Leia and Luke, after she buried their lightsabers near Luke's desert home. When she had first come to them, she was a nobody. But they had embraced her and helped shape her into a somebody. They were her family and she was theirs. The yellow-bladed lightsaber she had built would honor their legacy.

Once there was the Force, an energy field that surrounded and bound all living things. It had a dark side, and it had a light, and the tension between them maintained a balance. For a time the balance was upset and all seemed dark. But then came those who dared walk the skies to face the darkness and find a light.

The Force will be with them, always.

AUTHOR'S NOTE

MY DAD TOOK ME to see *Star Wars* on the day the space shuttle *Columbia* first launched, and from then I spent an entire childhood dreaming of the galaxy far, far away. If you told my younger self that I'd be involved in writing the sequels to the stories that were so much of my life back then, he'd probably nod and say, "Just make them good, please."

I've worked hard to fulfill that challenge and maybe even spark the imaginations of a new generation of kids who love these stories as much as I do.

What's wonderful about *Star Wars* storytelling is that it's a collaborative endeavor. Thanks to Michael Siglain for giving me the opportunity of a career to write the trilogy to end trilogies, and Jennifer Heddle for holding the glowrod high during ventures through regions unknown and being the most supportive of editors. And high praise is deserved for my comrades Alan Dean Foster, Jason Fry, and Rae Carson, who were fantastic companions on this journey and whose books show the power and beauty of telling these stories from another point of view.

Last of all, I'd like to thank my parents for encouraging their son to imagine the further adventures of Luke Skywalker, and my wife, Sandhya, for taking care of me in this galaxy while I labored away in another. This book was written with all youngling readers in mind, especially one who has recently joined our world, Sarina Isabel.

Go walk the skies, sweetheart. I'll be here for you. I promise.

ABOUT THE AUTHOR

MICHAEL KOGGE'S original work includes *Empire of the Wolf*, an epic graphic novel about werewolves in ancient Rome. He has penned books for many universes, from Harry Potter and Fantastic Beasts to *Game of Thrones* and *Batman v Superman*, and is most notably the author of the best-selling junior novels for *The Force Awakens*, *The Last Jedi*, and the *Star Wars Rebels* animated series.

He can be found online at www.MichaelKogge.com.